THE PALIMPSESTS

Aleksandra Lun

THE PALIMPSESTS

Translated from the Spanish by
ELIZABETH BRYER

A Verba Mundi Book
DAVID R. GODINE, *Publisher* · BOSTON

This is a *Verba Mundi* Book
published in 2019 by
David R. Godine, *Publisher*, Inc.
Post Office Box 450
Jaffrey, New Hampshire 03452
www.godine.com

Originally published in Spanish in 2015 by
Editorial Minúscula.
Copyright © Aleksandra Lun, 2015
English translation © Elizabeth Bryer, 2019
Translator's note © Elizabeth Bryer, 2019

LIBRARY OF CONGRESS CATALOGING-IN-PUBLICATION DATA

Names: Lun, Aleksandra, 1979- author. | Bryer, Elizabeth, 1986- translator.
Title: The palimpsests / Aleksandra Lun ; translated from the Spanish by
Elizabeth Bryer.
Other titles: Palimpsestos. English
Description: Boston : David R. Godine, Publisher, 2019. | "A Verba Mundi
Book." | Translated into English from Spanish. | Summary: "In *The Palimp-
sests*, Aleksandra Lun's debut novel, we find Przęśnicki, an Eastern-European
immigrant novelist who writes in Antarctic, languishing in a Belgium asylum,
undergoing Bartlebian therapy to strip away his knowledge of any language
that is not his native tongue. *The Palimpsests*, an absurdist comedy, is timely
in its relevance to today's discussions about immigration, senses of cultural
belonging and ownership, and personal relationships to language. Peppered
with darkly comic cameos from famous writers like Vladimir Nabokov, Samuel Beckett, Joseph Conrad, and of course, Przęśnicki's former lover Ernest
Hemingway."— Provided by publisher.
Identifiers: LCCN 2019023655 | ISBN 9781567926521 (trade paperback)
Classification: LCC PQ7061.P7 L8613 2019 | DCC 863/.7--dc23
LC record available at https://lccn.loc.gov/2019023655

FIRST PRINTING, 2019
Printed in The United States of America

*It would be more reasonable of me not to get involved in
drastic issues because I find myself at a disadvantage.
I am a completely unknown foreigner, I have no authority,
and my Spanish is a small boy who can barely speak.*

WITOLD GOMBROWICZ
"Against Poets"

1

M Y NAME is Czesław Przęśnicki, I'm a miserable Eastern-European immigrant and a failed writer, I haven't engaged in sexual relations for some time, and I've been committed to an asylum in Belgium, a country that has had no government for the past year. The reasons I find myself hemmed in by the cold walls of a psychiatric hospital in the north of Europe are as mysterious to me as the failure of my sex life, which has had me languishing in apathy and frustration for years. When I was born thirty-five years ago behind the Iron Curtain in the confusing geo-political space marked by Adolf Hitler's hyperactivity, nothing foretold that I would end up in a Belgian asylum one day. To be precise, the state that issues my passport is Poland, country of globe-trotting popes, frigid temperatures, and muscular war heroes among whom, hypocrisy aside, I don't count myself. I have a submissive nature, a flaccid body, and am thinning on top, and my faint-hearted self falls a long way short of exuding sex appeal for healthful fellow specimens of the male sex, whether under totalitarian regimes or democracy. Before I was committed to the psychiatric hospital of Liège, a city located in francophone Belgium, I lived in Vinson, the capital of Antarctica, where I shared the sad destiny of other miserable Eastern-European immigrants who set foot on that white continent clutching their newly acquired passports. That was how I learned Antarctic, a language I now speak fluently, though with a strong foreign accent, which I employed to write my first novel, *Wampir*, a critical and commercial failure.

Despite having published a book, I never wanted to be a writer but a veterinarian, and I can only blame the injustice of fate for the fact that I haven't been able to follow my one true calling. Perhaps that noble profession would have led me down other paths in life and, instead of now finding myself confined to an asylum writing a novel, I would be engaged in activities more constructive than literature. Yet we writers write for reasons that spring from our moral turpitude, to wit: ambition, an inflated ego, anguish, a desire to shine, arrogance, and fear of death. These dramatic circumstances spur our progress on the stories we present to our readers, innocent and generous souls who pay out of their own pockets to bestow on us a few hours of their lives. We tend to disappoint them because, as goes for the entire human race, among which weak and depraved examples of the species predominate, those of us who write badly far outnumber those who write well.

But my dream has always been to be a veterinarian, and throughout my communist childhood there was nothing to suggest that one day, instead of working in a clinic packed with unvaccinated dogs, I would be confined to an asylum in Belgium, a country that has had no government for the past year. Back then the days behind the Iron Curtain passed without incident, and as the years went by I devoted myself to lining up to buy toilet paper and fantasizing about attaining a passport. Everything got complicated when the Wall fell and we citizens of communist countries, until then habituated to the daily hunt for essential items, had to face the vast universe of possibilities that was the free market. Vices and debauchery came to Poland along with the Western multinationals, and in those new geopolitical circumstances I fell in love with a US citizen named Ernest Hemingway. Ernest, who was in Poland teaching boxing lessons in a school in Cracow, likewise took an interest in my flaccid self, and not long after we moved in together. Hemingway and I were very poor and very happy in our Cracowian flat, but the following year Ernest was offered a chance to teach boxing at the University of Vinson, the capital of Antarctica. Given my devotion to sex, I followed Hemingway to the white continent, where, due to the dearth of places in veterinary sciences, I enrolled in Antarctic language and literature. In Vinson we led a quiet life until the day Ernest upped and shot himself, leaving me nothing but a confusing farewell letter about a lost generation, the restroom of a Parisian bar, the two world wars, the Spanish Civil War, and a young soldier who tried to escape by bicycle. I spent the months following Ernest's suicide listening to Maria Calla's performance of Bellini's aria *Casta diva*, reading Nietzsche, and for the first time contemplating the concept of eternal return, never suspecting that it would prove untrue with respect to the future prospects of my sex life.

Despite all this I remained in Vinson and some years later graduated with a degree in Antarctic language and literature, not because I was interested in literature but because I had a student visa and so needed to continue studying to avoid being ousted from the country. What I was interested in was learning languages, for I nurtured the hope that speaking Antarctic and another language would not only help me integrate abroad but would also make me a polyglot or a happy person. Nothing could be further from the truth, given that for some time I've found myself languishing in sexual abstinence and confined to an asylum in a country that has had no government for the past year. The few pleasant moments I experience in the Liège psychiatric hospital are those I devote to my second novel, which I started writing on some old pages of the Flemish daily *De Standaard*. I found this Dutch-language newspaper beneath my bed and at first I used it in the absence of another medium but, in time, filled as it was with words in a language I can't understand, it ended up tranquilizing me more effectively than the medication the aides provide.

This was because for many years I thought, in line with the social propaganda I absorbed from a tender age, that speaking foreign languages was a cultural treasure, a privilege, and a stroke of luck. I had read several quotations on the subject by admired intellectuals such as Goethe, who said a man is worth as many men as foreign languages he possesses, and he who does not know a foreign language knows nothing of his own. Today I know that, apart from writing literary works, Johann Wolfgang studied the intermaxillary bone, but he was not the only one who bombarded me with irrefutable arguments in support of learning foreign languages. Education ministries and universities also assured unsuspecting citizens that speaking languages was a guarantee of both professional success and a satisfying personal life. I myself believed in those tall tales for years, realizing too late that speaking foreign languages leads to madness and that those who speak languages end up unhinged. Suffice it to consider the fate of the multilingual Karol Wojtyła, who spent years traveling the world draped in a white dress and living in the most touristy spot in Rome. While the worst that can happen to one who doesn't speak languages is being served the wrong dish in a restaurant abroad, the opposite scenario can mean ending up in the Vatican or being shut away in an asylum. At this stage of my miserable life I know that speaking languages only leads to bitterness and for this reason I am writing my second novel on some old pages of the Flemish daily *De Standaard*, Dutch being a language I don't know and one that therefore inspires in me tranquility and peace of mind.

I had to stop writing because my roommate, Father Kalinowski, finished his evening prayer, slipped off his cassock, blessed me, and switched off the light. Before being committed to the Liège psychiatric hospital, the priest lived in a block of flats in a mining town in the south of Poland and, aside from celebrating mass, he tended an allotment garden on the outskirts, where his five chickens pecked out an existence. Father Kalinowski is in the asylum due to a mysterious collapse he doesn't wish to talk about, and he spends his days praying, training on the stationary bicycle we have in our room, and listening to the radio, which he tunes to the Polish episcopacy station. Our cohabitation is difficult due to both the insomnia that torments the priest at night and his frequent prayers for the salvation of my soul, which he tends to carry out in the middle of our modest living space. Today he has fallen asleep and I have lain awake a long time, listening to his quiet breathing and fantasizing about leaving the Liège psychiatric hospital one day, engaging in sexual relations once more, and devoting myself to comforting domestic animals in a small clinic on the outskirts of Vinson.

2

I WAS DREAMING about a man draped in a white dress who descended the steps of a plane again and again to kiss all sorts of airport tarmac when I was woken by the shrieks of Father Kalinowski, who, terrified, was babbling something about a dead bird. The aides promptly arrived, straitjacketed him, and carted him off to the asylum manager's office. The doctor is a renowned psychiatrist and sees patients in a cold office fitted with a fireplace, which often reverberates with moans in unidentifiable languages that echo from the neighboring treatment room. I undergo therapy with her too, and the goal of our sessions is to reconstruct my life story, which, instead of steering me towards operating on dogs with cataracts, led me to write a book in a foreign language. My novel, *Wampir*, which marked the beginning of my failed literary career in Antarctic, narrated the story of a vampire who worked as a technician at a ski resort. One afternoon he was trapped in a defective cable car dangling in the Swiss Alps; the rescue effort took several days, and the vampire spent the time reading a book that someone had left behind. When they freed him from the cable car, my protagonist lost his mind and sank his fangs into the necks of the search-and-rescue team, howling that he had become a vampiric reader.

Despite this interesting climax, my novel *Wampir* went unnoticed by the general public and only attracted the attention of native Antarctic writers, who attended the presentation of my book at a Vinson bookshop and gave me a beating. Judging by the shouts the illustrious men of letters emitted when they hurled me to the floor, they were outraged because, despite my strong foreign accent, I had written my book in their mother tongue. The sage intellectuals inflicted me with kicks, pricked me with their fountain pens, and said they were fed up with illegal writers who came to Antarctica to steal their jobs. I tried to explain that a given language doesn't belong to its native speakers alone and that we miserable immigrants can write too, but they kept striking me with their walking sticks and ended up hurling me into a vacant lot.

Today I think that if I had come to any constructive conclusions about the native Antarctic writers' assault I might not now be confined to a Belgian asylum in the care of a psychiatrist specialized in Bartlebian therapy. The name of the treatment I undergo in the Liège psychiatric hospital comes from Bartleby, the character created by US writer Herman Melville, whom I met after Hemingway's suicide. We never did grow close because each time I proposed we talk about us or engage in wild sex, he responded that he would prefer not to. He ended up boarding a whaling ship, travelling to a Pacific island, and spending a month among cannibals, according to what he told me in a confusing farewell letter that also made mention of a white whale. As with Hemingway's suicide, Melville's disappearance plunged me into desperation, and I spent months crooning the aria *Casta diva* and reading Schopenhauer, growing increasingly convinced that life, and above all sex life, was a stretch of gloomy longing and a torment.

The objective of Bartlebian therapy is linguistic re-integration, and its basic tenets were established by a psychiatrist from the Swiss hospital of Herisau, Doctor Pasavento, who in his essay "Bartleby and Co." spoke for the first time about writers who stopped writing. His research, published in a French scientific journal, led to the development of treatment protocols for those inflicted with foreign-writer syndrome. The therapy is divided into two phases and consists of analyzing the events that drove the patient into an asylum and making him forget the foreign language he adopted to write his books. To this end, the immigrant writer is subjected to psychoanalysis and linguistic isolation, during which he maintains sole contact with his mother tongue or a language other than the one that afflicts him. As my case demonstrates, Bartlebian therapy is an effective treatment, as after many months of confinement in the Liège psychiatric hospital I am already forgetting Antarctic, the language I employed to write my first novel, *Wampir*.

I wasn't able to keep writing because Father Kalinowski returned from his therapy session and alerted the aides, alleging that I was getting overexcited while pawing some old pages of *De Standaard* and muttering in a diabolical language. The aides straitjacketed me and carted me off to the doctor's office, where the doctor regarded me with her impassive eyes and said that health-sector resources in Belgium, a country that had had no government for the past year, were limited. Then she ignored some shrieks in an unknown language that carried from the treatment room and added that the hospital had agreed to take me in on the condition that I demonstrated a cooperative attitude and didn't jeopardize the communal living arrangements. I said nothing, and the doctor asked what I was writing on the old pages of a Dutch-language daily and if I was doing so in my mother tongue, Polish, for that would indicate improvement to the state of my mental health.

I looked towards the fireplace and answered that I was writing my second novel, which I had decided to title *Kaskader*, and that I could not fight the creative impulse in a place as linked to lunacy and literature as an asylum. The doctor made a note in her notebook and asked if I had not had quite enough, what with the failure of my first novel, and if I thought that a second book would make my literary career take off in the direction of success. I sipped a little of the water that the doctor keeps on her oak table for patients and answered that I had no intention of taking off in the direction of anywhere because my novel was doomed to failure. *Kaskader* was to be my final book and a failed project par excellence, for I was writing it in Antarctic, a language that in the Liège psychiatric hospital is headed, on a Bartlebian flight, for the depths of oblivion.

The doctor responded that she could not comprehend why we citizens of post-communist countries had complexes so great that we not only talked about our personal problems using pretentious metaphors but abhorred our mother tongues too. I replied that we certainly had complexes, for getting around in outmoded clothing and sporting moustaches for more than forty years would affect anyone, but at any rate we Polish persevere with our mother tongue. I reminded the doctor of the case of the most polyglot resident of the Vatican, Karol Wojtyła, who for many years strived to promulgate the language that Father Kalinowski probably speaks during his deep psychoanalytic sessions.

From the treatment room came a pained moan, and the doctor regarded me with her impassive eyes, looked over her notes, and asked if my second novel was about a vampire too. I responded that *Kaskader* was the story of a Polish stunt double who leaps into the void by day, standing in for lead actors during action-film shootings, and writes a novel in an astronomical observatory by night. The doctor made a note in her notebook, got up, and called one of the aides, who gave me an injection and accompanied me to my room.

The medication depleted me but even so I intended to keep writing, and when Father Kalinowski tuned the radio to the live broadcast of a mass being celebrated in the Warsaw cathedral, my nerves betrayed me a little. I hurled the radio to the floor, and the priest blessed me and proposed we pray together so that God would give us back the good sense we had lost before being committed to the asylum. I recalled a few of Luis Cernuda's verses, I thought about how we foreign writers roam from one language to the next like dogs with cataracts, I jumped onto the table and shouted, "But there are no kindly gods who will return to us what we've lost, only blind chance which goes on tracing crookedly, like a staggering drunk, the stupid course of our lives!"

Then I slipped off my nightshirt and, when Father Kalinowski looked away and crossed himself, I got down from the table and into bed, a desolate place that serves as a daily reminder of the sad existence of my flaccid self. I lay there until nightfall and, when the priest switched off the radio and the light, I closed my eyes, hoping to fall asleep into an erotic dream about an alluring veterinarian.

I don't know what time I woke for I heard someone calling me and when I opened my eyes I saw Father Kalinowski sitting on the floor, resting his back against my bed. The room was dark, and I pretended I was still asleep, but the priest sighed and said he knew I was awake and he couldn't sleep either. I thought he wanted to tell me about the mysterious collapse that had brought him to the Liège psychiatric hospital and I let out an indifferent groan to convey my scant interest in night-time conversations with men who had made vows of chastity. Father Kalinowski switched on the headlamp he was wearing on his forehead and said he couldn't sleep because he was thinking about the canary that escaped from him when he was a boy. He had taken the cage up to the rooftop of his block of flats so the bird could see the city and its mines from above, but the canary managed to escape and some sparrows pecked it to death. A few hours later little Father Kalinowski found its lifeless body near the radio tower where, the day before World War II began, Hitler had organized a border incident to justify the invasion of Poland.

I responded that this happened to everyone, as hyperactive Hitler had organized many things, but could he please try not to dwell on his personal problems and instead get to sleep, for we had a difficult day ahead of us. The priest sighed, blessed me, switched off the headlamp, and went back to bed, where he started praying the Our Father. I lay awake a long while, reminiscing about the time I spent with Ernest Hemingway, the only man with whom I had, until that evening, spoken in a dark room. I never did grow close to Stefan Zweig, who at first was too busy writing *The Royal Game* and later committed suicide in Brazil, leaving me with nothing but a confused farewell letter insisting that Europe was destroying itself. After his death I spent months singing *Casta diva*, reading Spinoza, and coming to terms with the fact that the wisdom of a free man was not a meditation on death but on life, including sex life. From Father Kalinowski's bed came even breaths, and my thoughts turned to his corpulent torso, which I observed daily when he removed his cassock; I mused that his celibacy had certain benefits and fell asleep.

3

I DREAMED about a man draped in a white dress who, from the steps of a plane, blessed me in different languages for not having a sex life, and when I woke Father Kalinowski was training on the stationary bicycle. The priest blessed me with a smile, stopped pedaling, and left for his therapy session with the doctor. I got up, grabbed the old pages of *De Standaard*, and started working on *Kaskader*, but couldn't call to mind a few adjectives in Antarctic. I burst into tears, got back into bed, and realized that if the Bartlebian therapy proved effective it was unlikely I would finish my second and final book. Each time I asked myself why, instead of clipping the claws of innocent puppies, I was in an asylum writing a novel in a foreign language, I thought of Inspector Rex, the dogged detective. That likeable German shepherd was the protagonist of an Austrian TV show that during my student years screened every afternoon on a Vinson local network. In the show the noble animal solved all kinds of enigmas, mysteries, and police investigations, and signed court rulings and European arrest warrants with its powerful paws. Inspector Rex, the dogged detective, would not rest its wise canine head on its modest dog blanket until the last of the dangerous criminals was locked away in an Austrian prison reminiscent of the cold walls that hem me in at present. Together with the Polish writer Witold Gombrowicz, Inspector Rex, the dogged detective, is one of the mammals I most admire, and I mention this honest quadruped because in the asylum I've come to the conclusion that languages that are not our mother tongues are like cats.

Anyone will understand why I don't compare foreign languages to dogs by visualizing the behavior of one of those noble warm-blooded animals when its master arrives home after a long absence. In most cases the animal in question will start jumping, barking, and licking any exposed skin, and will then launch into other acts, maybe of a submissive nature but generally pleasant, with the sole objective of demonstrating its ability to remember. Numerous hounds behave in the same vein when they commit suicide on their masters' graves, where, throughout the days or weeks leading up to their own heroic deaths, they remain immobile, not drinking or eating solids. Others opt to go on living but spend the rest of their days heading to the office to search for their master even though he's dead, thus demonstrating not only eternal love but very little acumen too. Dogs are the stereotypical image of faithfulness and for this reason can only represent the mother tongue and not a foreign language, which ignores the individual with the cruelty of a cat or a totalitarian system. No cat or foreign language ever wastes time with someone who neglects to worship it daily, and only mother tongues and dogs can defy oblivion, the abuse of power, and totalitarianism.

I understood this to be the case one winter afternoon in Poland in the 1980s while, along with a hundred other fellow citizens of the communist system, I was lining up to buy toilet paper. During the communist period waiting in line was not only a response to the shortage of essential items but also a social activity that led to the formation of many marriages and, in the case of the lines for the most popular items, the conception of several children too. The years when essential items were scarce were also years of excessive sex for, in the absence of passports, personal freedom, and future prospects, Polish citizens devoted themselves wholeheartedly to it. This totalitarian luxury, which statisticians correlate with the coming of reproductive age of Polish nationals born at the end of World War II, caused the demographic explosion of the seventies, of which I myself am a faint-hearted fruit.

That day, the line I was in led out of a utopian supermarket, an establishment of a masochistic character common in Eastern Europe under the communist yoke. These were inhospitable places, empty not only of clients but of products too, locales where plastic one-liter bags of milk reigned as one of the few items available on a daily basis behind the Iron Curtain. These utopian supermarkets were governed by lady shop assistants, creatures who were barely human and flaunted moustaches, improbable perms, and pride in representing power. However much has been said about the terror that the communist authorities wreaked on the population in those years, those who truly wielded power behind the Iron Curtain weren't the party leaders but the lady shop assistants, who enjoyed unlimited access to toilet paper.

Ahead of me in the queue stood a skeletal man who often roamed the neighborhood clutching a bottle of the cheapest vodka, accompanied by an energetic black dog that had one floppy ear and a mischievous twinkle in its eyes. The three of us were in the stretch of the queue that was outside the utopian supermarket, a location that required mental toughness owing not only to the ruthless weather conditions in Eastern Europe, but also to the limited likelihood of reaching the counter in time. After we had spent several hours waiting, *Homo sovieticus*, buttressed with a moustache and an improbable perm, left the supermarket, cast a haughty glance in our direction, and shrilled with satisfaction that they were out of toilet paper. Accustomed to the lady shop assistants' rigidity of mind and mane, we utopian customers began to disperse without a word of complaint, and the skeletal man was the only one who didn't cower before totalitarian power incarnate. Emboldened by what remained in the bottle he held in his left hand, he raised it, paused a moment in a Napoleonic pose, and exclaimed in a voice shot through with pain and hope:

"Miss! At least one roll! It's not even for me...!" And using the hand that held the bottle, inside of which the dregs of the distinguished liquid were sloshing in melancholy, he gestured towards his quadruped friend, which from beneath its floppy ear looked at the lady shop assistant with a mischievous twinkle in its eyes.

I had to carry on with my search for toilet paper elsewhere, so I'm not sure whether the heart of *Homo sovieticus* softened at the prospect of depriving the skeletal hero's canine escort of an essential item. Most importantly, that was the day I realized I wanted to be a veterinarian, and only the passion I felt for Ernest

Hemingway diverted me from the life path I hope to return to someday. As for my canine metaphor for the mother tongue, the spectacle of a dog's faithfulness playing out against the devastated backdrop of a totalitarian regime devoid of toilet paper is further proof of its aptness. But foreign languages are like cats, and the elusive nature of those animals, which I have come to know as much through the scratches they have dealt me as through the dramatic testimonies of others, is the reason my Antarctic is headed, in the asylum, on a Bartlebian flight for the depths of oblivion.

I had to stop writing because Father Kalinowski, who had returned from his therapy session, alerted the aides on seeing me walking on all fours, invoking a certain Rex, and emitting noises he struggled to associate with any known mammal, much less a companion animal. Worried that I had been possessed by a demon, Father Kalinowski told the aides that my condition had worsened and that it saddened him to have to see me on a daily basis. This was not only because I stored expired condoms in my toiletry bag, but also because I had been occupying the bathroom at length, only to vacate it hours later with some old newspaper in hand.

"What must he be going through, the poor thing," a heavyhearted Father Kalinowski said to the aide who gave me the injection, "not even to realize that we stopped lining up to buy toilet paper back in '89."

4

THE MEDICATION had taken effect and I woke the next morning after dreaming all night about Inspector Rex, the dogged detective, who, draped in a white dress, wrote a book in a foreign language with the powerful paws of an Austrian shepherd. When I opened my eyes, Father Kalinowski smiled from his perch on the stationary bicycle and continued listening to the broadcast of one of Karol Wojtyła's visits to Poland. My nerves betrayed me a little and when the priest blessed me I got up, pulled off my nightshirt, got on top of the table, and started reciting some of Nicanor Parra's verses.

"I've got nothing left to say," I exclaimed in a threatening tone, and Father Kalinowski averted his eyes and turned up the radio. "Nobody answers my questions," I added as loudly as the ceiling was high, and the priest crossed himself and turned up the volume again.

The radio was broadcasting the pilgrimage to Karol Wojtyła's tomb in the Vatican and one of the priests, as he walked, lambasted sex practiced for any purpose other than procreation. I got down from the table, opened the window, and shouted at the top of my lungs:

"Abyss: respond at once!"

Father Kalinowski looked at me with concern, blessed me, and turned up the radio to the max, and when religious songs by a child choir rang out with full force I started kicking the door.

The aides straitjacketed me and carted me off to the

doctor's office, where shrieks of pain in unrecognizable languages carried from the treatment room. The psychiatrist regarded me with her impassive eyes and asked why I created conflicts in a hospital financed with the modest means of a country that had had no government for the past year. Then she consulted her notes and asked me to explain who Rex was, and I drank a little water and summarized my canine–feline metaphor. The doctor asked me why I didn't make the most of the evident advantages of writing in my mother tongue, rather than torment myself thinking up comparisons to the animal kingdom. She consulted her notes again and said that even Witold Gombrowicz, who had lived in Argentina for many years and whom I said I admired, wrote his books in Polish.

I answered that Polish was the language of not only Gombrowicz, but other people I admired too, such as eighties singer Danuta Lato, whose unnerving bosom helped me discover my sexual orientation. The doctor made a note in her notebook and I took nervous sips at the water again and added that she should be happy I wrote in Antarctic and not in Polish. Slavic languages, with the freedom proffered by their declensions, presented an added difficulty for the writer faced with a blank page, for if an Antarctic writer was met with innumerable possibilities, then a Polish writer came up against infinity. If I wrote in my mother tongue I would grow even more anxious when faced with a blank page and it was not in my interest to get anxious, given that I was dependent on the health sector of a country that had had no government for the past year.

The doctor made a note in her notebook and said if I couldn't stop writing in a foreign language perhaps I could stop writing, and my nerves betrayed me a little. I ran over to the bookshelf lined with diagnostic manuals and pulled it over, and at that moment in the corridor there was a sharp sound and the office door swung open, revealing a bald man who had boxing gloves on both fists.

"Mr. Nabokov," the doctor regarded him with her impassive eyes, "return to your room or I'll call the aides."

Vladimir Nabokov approached the table and gave the timber surface a punch.

"So foreigners, eh?" He regarded the psychiatrist with fury. "Foreign to what, to literature?"

The doctor failed to respond, and Nabokov gave the table another punch and shouted louder:

"And what are you going to do with us literary immigrants? Kick us out of your nation of native writers?"

"Nobody is going to kick you out of the hospital."

"Of course not out of here!" Nabokov punched the timber with both fists.

"You're not about to let us out of here to start writing novels in foreign languages!"

He gave the table a kick.

"Because we're the nutcases, and the sane ones are you and your mother tongues, right?"

The writer landed another kick and the table broke in two.

"Because we're the illegal writers and you hold citizenship in the nation of native literature, right?"

The doctor cast a furtive glance at the office door.

"No one's coming," Nabokov threw one of the table legs into the fireplace, where it started to blaze. "No one's coming because I've knocked out the aides."

The writer approached the psychiatrist, and I started backing towards the exit.

"What do you want from me?" shouted Nabokov. "Want me to spend all day talking to that Russian you put in my room? What? What more do you want? Want to box?"

I tripped and fell on the floor. Nabokov ran over and from the height of his muscular baldness glowered at me.

"And who's this?"

"Czesław Przęśnicki, another writer. Polish." The doctor regarded us with her impassive eyes.

Nabokov knelt down and brought one of his boxing gloves close to my face.

"So another Polish writer, eh? And, what, you write about wars and communism too?"

I burst into tears and answered that no I did not write about communism at all but about a Polish stunt double who leaps into the void during action-film shootings by day and writes a novel in an astronomical observatory by night.

"Voids are pretentious," the writer menaced me with his fist. "And the language?"

I was still sobbing on the floor.

"Language! What language do you write in!" Nabokov squashed my thinning hair with his boxing glove.

"In Antarctic," I murmured.

"Antarctic," muttered the writer and closed his eyes.

"Very well. You'll see that the transition from one language to another is the slow journey at night from one village to the next with only a candle for illumination."

He opened his eyes, withdrew the boxing glove from my head and inspected it. Then he looked at me with a penetrating gaze.

"Look, er..."

"Przęśnicki," I whimpered from the floor.

"Look, Przęśnicki," Nabokov fixed his gaze on his boxing glove once again. "I've been trilingual since I was a kid. But going from writing in Russian to writing in English was exceedingly painful – like learning anew to handle things after losing seven or eight fingers in an explosion."

Nabokov quit looking at the boxing glove, sprang to his feet, and ran towards the doctor.

"Bartlebian therapy! What do you know about Bartleby!"

"What culture do you belong to, Mr. Nabokov?" The doctor regarded him with her impassive eyes. "Russia? France? Great Britain? The United States?"

Nabokov stopped in his tracks before the psychiatrist.

"What do you care!" he roared and brought the boxing gloves up close to the doctor. "My head speaks English and my heart speaks Russian! And my ear, French!"

"You're a writer," the psychiatrist was making a note in her notebook, "you have to belong to a culture. All writers belong to one."

Nabokov was silent for a while and then raised both fists.

"The writer's art is his real passport!" he roared, and

through the door came one of the aides, who jabbed one syringe in the writer's muscular right arm and another in my flaccid left one.

The medication must have been strong because I woke a few hours later in my room, where Father Kalinowski was mending his cassock and listening to a Polish radio program about the rearing of free-range chickens. The priest blessed me with a smile, and his moustache reminded me of Joseph Stalin, the warm-hearted man I had seen in children's books patting happy pooches. Stalin said that language was a powerful weapon, and Vladimir Nabokov's boxing gloves perfectly illustrated this phrase of the man who cut short millions of men's lives. I preferred not to torment myself thinking about death and languages, and when Father Kalinowski switched off the light, I closed my eyes, hoping to dream about a veterinarian with a perfect body who devoted himself to caring for delicate foals by day and to wild sex by night.

5

I DREAMED the singer Danuta Lato and I were trapped in a cable car dangling in the Belgian Ardennes and, when I woke soaked in a cold sweat, Father Kalinowski had already left for his therapy session. I got up and tried on one of his cassocks, and the vision of my flaccid self concealed in the folds of that uncomfortable outfit seemed a gloomy omen for any future erotic activity. In one of the pockets I found the priest's headlamp, which I used to examine my privates, reflecting that it was unclear whether my sex life would ever return to the path it had strayed from so long ago. Then I hopped on the stationary bicycle, started pedaling, and mused that I didn't know if my literary career would get back on track either, when it hadn't even taken off with the publication of my first novel, *Wampir*. Perhaps the native Antarctic writers had a point the day they assaulted me at a book fair, dragged me outside by my thinning hair, and tortured me for hours in a garage. As they thwacked me with their manuscripts, the sage intellectuals blurted out that instead of writing books in foreign languages, we miserable immigrants should translate their exquisite creations into our own languages so they could exert some influence in our secondary cultures. When I called to mind the suffering that the native Antarctic writers visited on me, my nerves betrayed me a little and I got off the stationary bicycle, inserted the headlamp into my oral cavity, hoisted the pleats of the cassock, and jumped out the window.

It was cold in the hospital gardens but the aides soon arrived, straitjacketed me, and carted me off to the doctor's office, which Father Kalinowski was exiting right that moment. When the priest saw that I was wearing his cassock he smiled and blessed me as he passed by, and the doctor made no comment on my attire as she started looking over her notes. From the treatment room came thumping noises, and I drank a little of the water that sat on the small baroque table that the psychiatrist had substituted for the one Nabokov broke. The doctor regarded me with her impassive eyes, said that according to the Bartlebian therapy protocols we had to go back to the beginnings of my disorder, and asked me why I started writing.

I answered that my failed literary career started one winter's night when at two-thirty in the morning I was frying eggs for the Spanish writer Javier Cercas. I added that this was by no means to insinuate that the author of a book of five-hundred pages about a coup d'état would have been interested in my faint-hearted self, nor that he would have agreed to an encounter with me beyond the spiritual communion that typically occurs between writer and reader. The eggs were the subject of my labor in a bar in the Vinson city center, where soon after Ernest's suicide I started serving set meals to pay the rent. Cercas was in the Antarctic capital to present at a conference on his concept of the vampiric reader and, apart from the fried eggs, he ordered a beer and started reading an article by Mario Vargas Llosa. I lit the stove and decided to write, for while the oil heated in the frying pan it occurred to me that I had just made my entrance, via the kitchen door, into the pages of literary history.

The doctor made a note in her notebook, ignored a high-pitched shriek in an unidentifiable language that carried from the treatment room, and asked if on any other occasion it had occurred to me that I had made my entrance into the pages of literary history. I answered that the day my novel *Wampir* was published I'd had the same thought, but I ceased to think it when the publisher told me six copies had sold, four of which had been returned, one accompanied by a formal complaint.

The doctor called one of the aides, who gave me an injection and accompanied me to my room, where Father Kalinowski was singing a litany to the Black Madonna of Częstochowa. I told him that if he didn't cut the racket I would strip, and the priest crossed himself and answered that he didn't mind if I wore his clothes but could I please have some decency. I grabbed the old pages of *De Standaard* and went into the bathroom, but when I saw a photo of a smiling Karol Wojtyła by the mirror my nerves betrayed me a little. I went back into the room and tried to jump up onto the table but I got tangled in the cassock and fell and, when Father Kalinowski ran over to help me, I thought of Nietzsche and asked from the floor:

"Are we not plunging continually? Backward, sideward, forward, in all directions?"

The priest blessed me and I got up, pulled on the headlamp I had tucked into the pocket of the cassock, and switched it on.

"Do we not need to light lanterns in the morning? Do we hear nothing as yet of the noise of the gravediggers who are burying God?"

The priest crossed himself, and I exclaimed:

"God is dead! And we have killed him!" I hurled the headlamp to the floor and shut myself in the bathroom.

I spent the rest of the day writing *Kaskader* and sobbing each time I tried to construct the passive voice in Antarctic, and I only got into bed when Father Kalinowski was about to switch off the light. I visualized myself in the arms of a lustful veterinarian and soon fell asleep but was woken by the light of the headlamp being shone in my eyes. Father Kalinowski sat on the floor and said he knew I couldn't sleep and he couldn't sleep either, because he was thinking about a dead bird. Then he sighed and added that he was upset because the sparrows killed his canary in the same spot Hitler had used as a pretext for invading Poland.

I answered that this happened to everyone, for hyperactive Hitler invaded many countries, but could he please try to calm down and get to sleep because we had a difficult day ahead of us. Then I asked if he had spoken to the doctor about his personal problems, but the priest sighed once more and got into bed, and soon there came the sound of heavy snoring. I lay awake a long while in the darkness, thinking that, if only I too had made a vow of chastity, I might contemplate the abyss that was my sex life with similar serenity, until I fell asleep.

6

I woke shouting after dreaming that the protagonist of my first novel, the vampiric reader, got off a plane and kissed the tarmac of a military airport, only to be executed by a battalion of native Antarctic writers for the crime of reading with a foreign accent. When I opened my eyes, Father Kalinowski was performing an exorcism over me, and on seeing I was awake he blessed me and announced that he had washed the cassock in case I needed to wear it. Then he got onto the stationary bicycle and started pedaling, and I grabbed the old pages of *De Standaard*, shut myself in the bathroom, and started to write. I recalled his night-time confession and realized his torment must have sprung from the fact that the Liège psychiatric hospital was located near the site of the Battle of the Bulge, part of the offensive that hyperactive Hitler launched at the end of 1944. Kurt Vonnegut participated in the military operation, yet we never did grow close as, a few days after we met, he disappeared from my life without the least explanation. Later, the US writer sent me a confusing letter from Dresden explaining that when he participated in the Battle of the Bulge, he got separated from his battalion and roamed the woods until he was captured by the Germans. In Dresden, he survived the Allies' bombardments and spent several days piling bodies that were so numerous they had to be burned with flamethrowers. Vonnegut said he was going to describe it in a novel and had heard that a certain Sebald wanted to pen a book about the German cities razed by bombardments too. Over the following months, I focused on listening to *Casta diva*, reading Wittgenstein, and accepting that, even if one day all the questions posed by science were answered, those answers wouldn't scratch the surface of the true problems of life, especially sex life.

Father Kalinowski spent the morning training and I kept working on *Kaskader*, but I ended up bursting into tears because I wasn't sure about the gender of several nouns in Antarctic. At midday, I went to the doctor's office, and she asked me how long I intended to keep writing in a foreign language and taking advantage of the limited resources of a country that had had no government for the past year. I didn't answer and sipped a little water, and the doctor read over her notes and asked me what happened after I dished up the fried eggs for Javier Cercas.

From the treatment room came a pained moan, and I shuddered and said that when my shift finished that night and I arrived home I started writing my first novel, *Wampir*. The doctor regarded me with her impassive eyes and made a note in her notebook, and I added that my book's publication marked the beginning of my persecution at the hands of the native Antarctic writers. On remembering the suffering that the illustrious men of letters inflicted on me, my nerves betrayed me a little, and I hurled the glass of water to the ground and ran to the office door. Before I could open it, a man with greying hair and a penetrating gaze, armed with a cricket bat and accompanied by a man wearing a woolen jersey, opened it from the corridor.

"Czesław Przęśnicki?" The man looked down his nose at my thinning hair and, not waiting for a response, introduced himself: "Samuel Beckett, at your service."

He strode into the office and struck the small baroque table with the cricket bat, causing it to collapse.

"Samuel Beckett, at your service," he repeated, looking at the psychiatrist, who made a note in her notebook.

"No need to introduce yourself, Mr. Beckett."

"Samuel Beckett, at your service." The writer struck the remains of the small table again. "And this," he extended the hand clutching the cricket bat towards the man in the woolen jersey, "is Jerzy Kosiński."

"At your service," Kosiński said from the doorway.

Beckett approached the doctor, and I tiptoed towards the exit.

"Stay there, Jerzy. Nobody is to come in or out." Beckett sat in my chair and, not letting go of the cricket bat, lit a cigar.

"Well, well, Nabokov told us everything," he exhaled the smoke towards the doctor. "This poor specimen," he pointed at me with the Cuban cigar, "is writing a novel in Antarctic and you treat him as if he's unhinged. Am I right, Przęśnicki?"

I nodded and burst into tears, and the doctor regarded Beckett with her impassive eyes.

"You, Mr. Beckett? You, advising more people to write in foreign languages? Can't you see where writing in French has led you?"

Beckett threw the cigar to the floor and crushed it with his shoe. "Of course I can. It's led me to an asylum!" He exchanged a look with Kosiński and let out a diabolical laugh. "We're mad!" Beckett stopped laughing. "We are all born mad. Some remain so." He hit what was left of the small baroque table with the cricket bat once more. "Jerzy!"

"Samuel?" responded Kosiński from the door.

"Tell her where you're from."

"I'm a Polish Jew, at your service."

"Occupation?" Beckett was playing with the cricket bat and looking sidelong at the psychiatrist.

"Writer," answered Kosiński, and Beckett made a gesture of impatience and got up from the chair.

"Your language, Jerzy, your language. Tell her what language you write in."

"Jerzy Kosiński, English-language writer, author of *The Painted Bird*, at your service."

"Well, well," Beckett was peering at the psychiatrist, "so a painted bird, doctor."

He started pacing around the office.

"So a man paints some birds all different colors, releases them, and watches on while other birds peck them to death."

He stopped before the fireplace.

"So a dark-haired boy wanders about small villages in Eastern Europe during World War II."

The doctor regarded Kosiński with her impassive eyes.

"What gives you the idea that you can invent whatever you feel like and write it in any language you fancy?"

"A writer, doctor," Kosiński shrugged his shoulders, "is issued a special license, a poetic one, and that license is good for his own life too."

The doctor made a note in her notebook.

"If I wrote in my mother tongue," continued Kosiński, "what I wrote would become personal. I write in my stepmother tongue, so that it may be universal."

The doctor regarded us with her impassive eyes, and Beckett placed the cricket bat on the floor and sat down again.

"And what do you write about, Prześnicki?"

"About a Polish stunt double who leaps into the void during action-film shootings by day and writes a novel in an astronomical observatory by night." I looked at the floor.

"The part about leaping into the void is a little pretentious," the writer exchanged a glance with Kosiński, "but the most important thing is that you don't write in your mother tongue."

The doctor made a note in her notebook.

"The mother tongue is a tired concept!" shouted Beckett, getting out of his chair. "As tired as your Bartlebian therapy!"

He went over to the doctor and crouched beside her.

"You and your kind have never been foreigners, that's your bad luck," he lowered his voice, "and you don't know that the mother tongue is always burdened with automatism and that, to simplify things, exiling oneself from the language is necessary. Am I right, Jerzy?"

"Yes." Kosiński was still in the doorway. "But my English is like a bad-tempered lover. I can't leave her alone too long."

"That's why you're here. To write in your authentic language once more." The doctor regarded him with her impassive eyes.

"The same was said about me: that I abandoned my authentic language," Kosiński shrugged his shoulders, "and that I crossed over to another for the money. And that I didn't know English and *The Painted Bird* was written by the CIA."

I burst into tears.

"No hysterics, Przęśnicki." The writer looked me up and down, went over to the table, and grabbed the cricket bat from the floor. "In the state you're in, be sure not to write in your mother tongue. You'll find that the stepmother tongue is free of that emotional burden."

He swung the bat around in the air and asked if I played sport or had heard talk of painted birds, and I mumbled that my roommate's canary had been pecked to death by sparrows.

"Too foreign," Jerzy Kosiński looked at the doctor, who looked back at him with her impassive eyes, "too exotic to fly free."

The writer started walking towards the psychiatrist, cricket bat in hand.

"Do you believe, Doctor, that canaries sing with an accent?"

"Jerzy!" Beckett grabbed him by the woolen jersey. "Come off it. Let's hear what Przęśnicki has to say about his book."

Kosiński halted, and I swallowed saliva and said that *Kaskader* was my second and final book and that the first was *Wampir*, a critical and commercial failure.

"It's all the same, Przęśnicki." Beckett headed towards the door, indicating to Kosiński that he should do the same. "Try again. Fail again. Fail better. But forget about mother tongues."

The writers left, after which the sounds of something heavy falling to the ground and shouts in several languages reached us from the corridor, and one of the aides entered the doctor's office with a syringe in hand. On seeing him coming towards me, my nerves betrayed me a little, and once he had made me spit out all the bits of one of the table legs I kicked him in the genitals. I tried to explain that if everyone wrote in the same language not only would all asylums have to be closed down, but so would all concentration camps and publishing houses, yet the aide only proceeded to straitjacket me. As he was emptying the syringe into my flaccid right buttock, I tried to touch his privates, but the medication had taken effect and I passed out.

7

I DREAMED that Karol Wojtyła, draped in a white dress, was motioning to me from a cable car dangling in the Tatra Mountains while I waited in a ski-resort cafeteria, where Maria Callas's performance of *Casta Diva* was blaring. I woke in the morning to the sounds of Father Kalinowski, who had his eyes closed and was down on his knees beside my bed, praying a novena for me. My nerves betrayed me a little, and when the aides arrived they straitjacketed me and carted me off to the doctor's office. The psychiatrist was looking over her notes behind a large desk, which had replaced the little baroque table that Samuel Beckett broke, and from the treatment room came drawn-out moans. She regarded me with her impassive eyes and asked me why, instead of putting my high-conflict personality on display, I didn't show gratitude for the resources placed at my disposal by a country that had had no government for the past year. I said nothing, and the doctor read over her notes and asked me why I didn't quit writing and try to become a veterinarian after my novel *Wampir* had failed.

I responded that the editor of my first book made the same suggestion after slapping me several times the day I went to beg his pardon and give him back the money he had lost on my novel. When I left the publishing house I decided to start a new life caring for worthy representatives of the animal kingdom and set out for the University of Vinson to enroll in veterinary studies. In the student registration office, I came upon the native Antarctic writers, who carted me off to an industrial site and walloped me with several research papers dedicated to analyzing their grandiose works. While they burned several copies of *Wampir*, they told me that we miserable immigrants should learn foreign languages not to write novels, but to organize free concerts featuring folkloric songs from our respective countries. Then they shoved me in the boot of a Ford Fiesta and took me to the Vinson International Airport, where they threw me to the floor and told me to go write books in foreign languages in some other country.

The doctor made a note in her notebook, and I sipped a little water and said that when I regained consciousness in the airport restroom, I decided to travel to the grave of Witold Gombrowicz. I had nowhere to go and thought that a posthumous encounter with one of the mammals I most admired would help me decide what to do with the rest of my miserable life. Gombrowicz was buried in Vence, the village in Provence where, after he departed Argentina and returned to Europe, he spent his final years. He died soon after leaving Buenos Aires, the city where, by sheer coincidence, he stepped off the ship a week before the Second World War broke out and stayed for more than twenty years.

The doctor regarded me with her impassive eyes, and I asked if she was familiar with the Vence photographs of Gombrowicz, which depicted the former frequenter of hovels and seedy bars posing in the lounge room of his elegant home, together with his young wife. In the photos taken in Provence, the one-time rebel of the literary periphery looks like a consecrated European writer in comfortable surroundings, someone who works at a table covered in books and entertains intellectual friends. The doctor said nothing, and I shuddered and added that the same Gombrowicz sensed that Europe would end up stifling him. Even so, he spent his mornings mocking his new lifestyle in his diary before stepping out to buy expensive clothing with the money won from a prestigious literary prize, telling his wife that true artists always went about incognito.

From the treatment room came painful weeping, and I swallowed saliva and said that, when the plane touched down in Nice, I set out for the bus station and hopped aboard a bus headed for Vence. I sat beside an elderly lady, attracted by the lost look in the eyes of her little dog, and I observed it with a sense of déjà vu until I realized its little white head reminded me of Psina, the dog that belonged to Gombrowicz. Psina often posed alongside the writer in the Vence photographs and, in one taken during an interview recorded for French radio, the dog stretches its head above the table and regards the camera with the gaze of an alienated intellectual. The little dog on the bus started sniffing me, and I thought it plausible that a writer would have a dog for even I, a failed writer, was fascinated by Rex, the dogged detective. When the little dog sneezed, I mused that the strange thing was that Psina was one of the few writers' dogs, if not the only one, whose photos continued to be published after its master's death.

The doctor looked at me with her impassive eyes and asked if I thought that dogs wrote novels in foreign languages, or that at some stage I'd met an intellectual dog. I sipped a little water and answered that I didn't think dogs were writers, even though many hounds I'd met had no sex life to speak of. The doctor made a note in her notebook, and I added that the rebellious presence of Psina in the photos, now sans Gombrowicz, was proof of that old belief that dog owners end up looking like their dogs. In any case, after the persecution I suffered at the hands of the native Antarctic writers, my encounter with what might have been a reincarnation of Psina seemed like a fateful sign, and I thought that Gombrowicz was trying to communicate with me from beyond the grave. But when the bus pulled into the Vence bus station, the supposed bearer of the soul of an exiled writer's dog looked at me sidelong and then proceeded to demonstrate a powerful sexual desire towards my left leg.

From the treatment room came drawn-out howls, and I said that when I managed to free myself from the powerful paws of the little white dog I stepped off the bus drenched in canine pheromones and headed for the Vence cemetery. I spent a long while gazing at Gombrowicz's grave, and the silence and physical proximity of the writer, though decomposed, ended up troubling me. I felt like talking to the master and, given that he lay a few, though decisive, meters underground, I sat on his grave and related to him the suffering inflicted on me by the illustrious Antarctic men of letters. When I took off my shirt and showed the grave of Gombrowicz the bruises that the sage intellectuals gave me when they battered me with their notebooks, I heard someone calling my name.

"Przęśnicki!"

I looked around but there was nobody else in the cemetery.

"Down here, Przęśnicki."

My nerves betrayed me a little, and when I stopped sobbing and asked who it was, a hoarse voice answered.

"Who do you think? Can't you see the name on the headstone?"

I asked in a soft voice if he'd heard what I'd said.

"Of course," responded Gombrowicz from beneath the marble, "you were howling like an abandoned dog."

Then he coughed again and shouted:

"Psina! Leave that bone alone, you'll get food poisoning!" He added: "You should play more sport, Przęśnicki. You're not in great shape."

I put my shirt back on, and some fierce barks rose from the grave.

"Look, Przęśnicki," Gombrowicz's voice sounded again, "sometimes, I'd like to send all writers abroad, out of their own language, and out of all ornament and verbal filigree, to see what would be left of them."

I murmured that I didn't know what would be left of the Antarctic writers if they were sent abroad but they definitely had it in for me, and that it was easy to give advice when you were dead and had written your books in your mother tongue.

"Don't be dramatic, Przęśnicki," Gombrowicz coughed beneath the headstone, "you know very well what I wrote in our mother tongue. And so many people really did have it in for me. And I wrote something in Spanish too. Read *Our Sexual Drama*."

I burst into tears and from below the headstone came several howls.

"Quiet, Psina!" shouted Gombrowicz before adding in a tranquil tone, "You're well aware, Pręśnicki, that in a foreign language you can't craft phrases that are potent, or agile, or distinguished, or delicate, but who knows, maybe this forced diet is good for one's health? What are you writing about?"

"About a Polish stunt double who leaps into the void during action-film shootings by day and writes a novel in an astronomical observatory by night," I murmured.

"Don't be dramatic, Pręśnicki, or you'll end up pretentious," coughed Gombrowicz.

From beneath the headstone came a drawn-out howl, and I swallowed saliva and asked Gombrowicz if he was sure his dog was alright.

"He'll be alright," I heard the writer exhaling smoke, "don't be dramatic. What's important is that you're caustic, Pręśnicki. Literature must be caustic."

Gombrowicz coughed again and I heard a familiar panting that announced the arrival of the vehicular reincarnation of Psina, which I sent flying over a cluster of bushes with the help of my right leg and the same gratuitous violence that I so often decry.

The doctor made a note in her notebook, and I said that when I realized I'd almost killed a representative of the same species as Rex, the dogged detective, I started to harbor serious doubts about the suitability of my faint-hearted self for the task of manipulating defenseless animals' innocent bodies. The psychiatrist called one of the aides, who gave me an injection and accompanied me to my room, where Father Kalinowski was praying along to the rosary being broadcast from the Wawel Cathedral.

The medication knocked me out and as the priest was blessing me I merely had the strength to howl like an abandoned dog. Father Kalinowski crossed himself and turned up the radio, and I asked him from bed:

"Do you think dogs go to heaven?"

The priest intoned the religious hymn playing on the radio, and before falling asleep I thought that the dogs that provided company for their masters when they were in exile or in line to buy toilet paper deserved for there to be a canine paradise.

I was woken by sharp pinches, and Father Kalinowski said he knew I couldn't sleep and he couldn't sleep either, because he was thinking about a dead bird. I responded that he had nothing to worry about, as a short time before a friend with whom I was thick as thieves told me that it was quite common for birds to get pecked to death for being different. The priest sighed and said he couldn't stop thinking about his canary, for not only was the spot where it had died close to the radio tower where World War II began, but it was also some forty kilometers from Auschwitz. I responded that this happened to a lot of people, as hyperactive Hitler constructed several concentration camps, but could he please try to rest because we had a difficult day ahead of us. The priest returned to his bed and I visualized a voluptuous, long-haired veterinarian; wondered whether I could become a sex stunt double, given that my sex life, just like my Antarctic, was headed for the depths of oblivion; and fell asleep.

8

I DREAMED that, while Hitler was preparing his false flag operation in the radio tower of a mining town, Gombrowicz was disembarking at the port of Buenos Aires, where native Polish writers started giving him a hiding for his lack of patriotism. I woke sobbing and when I opened my eyes saw Father Kalinowski, who was on his knees praying for the redemption of my sins before a new photo of a smiling Karol Wojtyła. I pulled the covers over my head and was reminded of the mornings I'd shared with Ernest before I thought about the writer Bruno Schulz, with whom I never did grow close because he disappeared from my life without even a farewell letter. Later I found out a Nazi killed him in the Drohobych ghetto and I spent months intoning *Casta Diva*, reading Ortega y Gasset, and accepting that the act of thinking was like dog-paddling to save oneself from damnation amid chaos or, in some cases, from an unsatisfactory sex life.

Father Kalinowski remained on his knees before Karol Wojtyła, and I grabbed a few pages of *De Standaard*, shut myself in the bathroom and started writing and sobbing each time I tried to conjugate an irregular verb in Antarctic. At midday I had my therapy session, and when I entered the office the psychiatrist was standing before the fireplace consulting her notes, while from the treatment room came shrieks in incomprehensible languages. I sat down and sipped a little water, and when the doctor took a seat at her desk and asked me what I decided to do after visiting Gombrowicz's grave, I answered, "Nothing." Awaiting me outside the cemetery were the native Antarctic writers, who were in Vence for a literary awards ceremony, and they proceeded to flog me with their scarves. The sage intellectuals asked why we miserable immigrants, instead of featuring in documentary footage about our countries' cuisines, insisted on writing novels in other languages and signing them with our exotic surnames. Then they threw me to the ground, dealt me several loafer-clad kicks, flattened me with their obese bodies, shoved a handkerchief in my mouth, and bundled me into a Ford Fiesta, where I passed out.

The doctor made a note in her notebook and asked if I often got the feeling that writers from other countries were pursuing me across several continents because I was their enemy. I swallowed saliva, looked at the fireplace, and said in a soft voice that we foreign writers were not native writers' enemies, but their doubles. To describe those doubles, who like the protagonist of my second novel would stand in for lead actors in action films, in Polish we had a more expressive word, which I had chosen as the title of my second novel, *Kaskader*. It was a more fitting word because its harsh sounds evoked a cascade of forward movement, a screeching of brakes, a cloud of dust, and a leap from a car that kept on towards the precipice. From the treatment room came a muffled roar and the doctor regarded me with her impassive eyes and asked at what point I had started to believe I was a *kaskader* of literature. I burst into tears and answered that it was when from the depths of an abyss I started writing my last novel in a language I was forgetting with the fury of one who has nothing to lose. I was writing my book in Antarctic in an asylum as if I were making love in a rented hovel for the last time ever, an act that tasted of vitality and ultimatum that native writers, like stable couples banging in their mortgaged flats, could never know.

The doctor called an aide, who gave me an injection and accompanied me to my room, where Father Kalinowski was sprinkling my bed with holy water. The priest blessed me, and I grabbed the pages of *De Standaard* and headed for the bathroom when I heard someone calling my name.

"Przęśnicki!"

I went to the window and spied a man dressed in black on an old racing bicycle in the hospital garden.

"Quick, Przęśnicki." The cyclist glanced around.

I opened the window and the man looked at Father Kalinowski, who was blessing my little cotton socks.

"Cioran." The cyclist held out his hand. "Beckett told me about you, Przęśnicki."

"Emil Cioran? The Romanian writer who writes in French?"

Cioran laughed.

"I have no nationality. I don't need a fatherland anymore. I don't want to belong to anything."

He glanced around once more, let the bicycle drop to the ground, and went over to the window.

"I don't have much time, Przęśnicki. Sometimes I escape my room to do a little sport."

He looked at the frost covering the garden and at

Father Kalinowski, who had prostrated himself in the form of a cross on the ground.

"Listen carefully, Pręśnicki," he raised his gaze to the sky. "Don't get swept up in Bartlebian therapy."

I nodded and burst into tears.

"Writing in a foreign language is an illuminating experience and, more to the point," Cioran continued gazing at the sky, "for a writer, to change language is to write a love letter with a dictionary."

Father Kalinowski got up, came over to the window, and blessed the both of us.

"In my case, Pręśnicki," Cioran went on, "it was difficult to write in French because by temperament the French language doesn't suit me. I need a savage language, a language of drunkards. French is a straitjacket."

"And what did the native French writers say about you?" I sobbed.

"Who cares what other writers say?" Cioran lowered his gaze. "The most interesting people are those who haven't written anything."

I kept sobbing and Cioran regarded me with his indifferent eyes.

"I know your metic complex, Pręśnicki. I started writing in French when I was thirty-seven. I'd never written anything in that language. Except letters to ladies, of course."

"I'm forgetting my Antarctic," I whimpered, and Cioran sighed and looked skyward again.

"We last as long as our fictions, Pręśnicki," he lowered his gaze and watched Father Kalinowski, who was hopping onto his stationary bicycle. "One way or another, you have to do more sport. Good health is the best weapon against religion. Or so they say."

He glanced around again and picked the bike up off the ground.

"I have to go. Hey, so what's this *kaskader* story about?"

"He is the protagonist of my novel in Antarctic, a Polish stunt double who leaps into the void during action-film shootings by day and writes a novel in an astronomical observatory by night." I looked at the ground.

"Leaps, voids, and abysses tend to be pretentious, Przęśnicki," Cioran hopped onto the bicycle, "but the important thing is that the book not be in your mother tongue, and that it be dangerous. Each book has to be dangerous."

He started pedaling and was gone.

That night Father Kalinowski blessed me sooner than usual and switched off the light, and I lay awake fantasizing about being trapped in a cable car swinging between two peaks in the Pyrenees with a lecherous veterinarian. I recalled Ernest and then Walter Benjamin, with whom I never did grow close because he committed suicide in Portbou while attempting to flee the Nazis. I spent months analyzing his suicide, singing along to *Casta Diva* with Maria Callas, and reading Hume's complete works. From Father Kalinowski's bed came the sounds of regular breathing, and I decided that I had to stop tormenting myself over my sex life, for nature would always maintain her rights and prevail in the end over any abstract reasoning, and fell asleep.

9

I DREAMED that during World War II Bruno Schulz lifted off in a cable car in the streets of a Galician city while several stray dogs howled all around him. When I woke Father Kalinowski stopped intoning a Gregorian chant, smiled at me, held out a chalice, and said it brought glad tidings. I closed my eyes once more, and the priest traced a cross on my forehead, said that if I needed his cassock I could take it, got down on his knees before the photo of a smiling Karol Wojtyła, and started singing a carol. I grabbed the pages of *De Standaard*, shut myself in the bathroom, and started writing, but when I heard shouts from Father Kalinowski, who was now praying the rosary, my nerves betrayed me a little. I opened the bathroom door and when the priest raised his eyes I stripped off my nightshirt and shouted some Lucretius verses.

"Fear in sooth holds so in check all mortals!"

The priest averted his eyes and blessed himself.

"Believing them therefore to be done by power divine!" I shouted louder, and Father Kalinowski regarded me with sorrowful eyes and blessed me. "Many operations go on in earth and heaven!" I flung my nightshirt at the priest. "The causes of which they can in no way understand!"

The doctor was waiting for me in her cold office and, as the aides removed my straitjacket, she asked me why it was that instead of trying to write in my mother tongue I insisted on being a constant source of problems for a country that had welcomed me with open arms, despite having had no government for the past year. Then she consulted her notes, ignored a drawn-out cry coming from the treatment room, and asked where the native Antarctic writers took me after finding me outside the cemetery in Vence. I sipped a little water and responded that when I regained consciousness, my hands and feet were tied, and I was in the backseat of a Ford Fiesta in the Nice airport parking lot. The illustrious intellectuals told me they were sick of immigrant writers, they were going to send me back to where I came from, and had booked me on a direct flight for Eastern Europe. With that, they dealt me several kicks and handed me a ticket to Bucharest, and when I tried to explain that Bucharest was in Romania, not Poland, they pummeled me with the first editions of their books.

From the treatment room came a protracted yowl, and I shuddered and said that the city where the native Antarctic writers sent me, the so-called Little Paris, would have appealed to Rex, the dogged detective. Around Bucharest roam masses of stray dogs that look not at all aimless but intelligent and enterprising, with personalities all their own and with the decisive strides of those who know exactly where they are running. Dogs in the Romanian capital are different from the dazed and cowardly canine specimens in other European cities, which watch from the heights of their sofas as the years of their decadent lives go by. Compared to their affluent Western counterparts, the dogs of Little Paris are like young entrepreneurs hailing from new tech startups vis-à-vis the pot-bellied, cigar-smoking sixty-somethings who sit on heavy-industry companies' management boards.

A few years ago, the Bucharest city council decided to eradicate the dogs, but the city's inhabitants, with the imagination of those who have learned to circumvent orders under communism, bought identification chips for as many quadruped comrades as they could. The initiative not only made the dogs untouchable in the eyes of the uncanine administration, but also gave rise to many stories of love between dogs with a past and owners who wanted to give them a future. For instance, when I was in the Jewish cemetery of Bucharest and saw the look that the gravedigger's dog gave its owner, I knew I was in the presence of a love come late in life. For despite its modest dimensions, worn-down teeth, and ridiculous little red vest, the gravedigger's canine companion had the contented look and honest face of an owner of a clandestine printing press.

The doctor made a note in her notebook and asked me why I went to a Jewish cemetery, and I answered that I wanted to see the grave of Adolf Hittler, who is buried in the Filantropia Cemetery in Bucharest. The psychiatrist asked if in that cemetery I'd likewise visited gratuitous violence upon some poor dog, and I said that I had not, but without intending to I fell on top of someone who, according to the gravestone, had been a veterinarian in his time. My unexpected horizontal position in a Jewish cemetery led me to engage in not only a quick ontological reflection, but also an involuntary sacrilege, which I committed on getting up from the grave. A few meters farther on I found the gravestone of Adolf Hittler, who died in Bucharest in 1892 at the age of sixty and who had made and sold hats in the city center. I did the math and

realized that when hatter Adolf Hittler was buried in the
Jewish cemetery in Little Paris, hyperactive Adolf Hitler
was three years old.

Several bellows carried from the treatment room,
and I asked the doctor if she knew the photographs of
Hitler in Paris, taken during the visit the dictator paid
one July morning in 1940 to the vacant City of Light
that had recently surrendered at his feet. The doctor
regarded me with her impassive eyes, and I said that
on his five-am stroll through somnolent Paris, Hitler
must have felt more than ever that he was following the
path of providence with the accuracy and sureness of a
sleepwalker. At some moment during that visit his silver
Mercedes would pass by a small hat shop, at which time
the chancellor of the Third Reich would be overcome
by a strange impulse, command the driver to stop, wind
down the window, and stare at a yellow hat in the display
that seemed to be shooting him a tilted smile. Seized by
sudden vertigo, Hitler would shout at the driver to step
on it, huddle in the backseat, and hold his breath until
the silver Mercedes carried him far from that Jewish hat,
which was transmitting via radiofrequency an irresist-
ible message from the past.

The doctor made a note in her notebook, and I said
that, when I was committed to the asylum and met Father Kalinowski, I remembered the words of William
Faulkner, who said that a book is the writer's secret life
and the dark twin of a man. And when I started to forget
Antarctic I decided to write *Kaskader* because I thought
that the story of a Polish stunt double would be my final
dark twin brother, alongside whom I would leap into

the void, stirring up a cloud of dust.

The doctor was about to ask me something when the door opened and in came a man sporting a beard and a sailor's cap.

"Ah, from the ship!" he exclaimed and gave my flaccid self a hug that smelled of distant ports. Then he let me go, waited for me to catch my breath, and looked at me with fatherly pride.

"Dear, dear Czesław. Cioran told me all about you."

"Exploring the lands beyond your room, Mr. Korzeniowski?" The doctor made a note in her notebook.

The sailor grabbed a chair, sat down beside me, took off his cap, and gently corrected the psychiatrist.

"Joseph Conrad, *madame*. After so long, you might endeavor to recall my name."

The doctor regarded him with her impassive eyes.

"And you might return to your room and write in your mother tongue. You're not in the jungle anymore."

"The most exotic jungle in the world is the human soul, *madame*."

The doctor refrained from answering, and Conrad smiled at me.

"Tell me about your book, son. What are you writing about?"

"About a *kaskader* who leaps into the void during action-film shootings by day and writes a novel in an astronomical observatory by night." I looked at the floor.

"Ah, from the ship!" Conrad stroked his beard. "And are you sure that your young man has to leap into the void, son?"

"Yes," I answered in a soft voice.

The writer regarded me with sympathetic eyes.

"But you write in Antarctic, right?"

I nodded and said that I hadn't made much progress because Father Kalinowski made a lot of noise and switched out the light very early.

"So you're also sharing your room with a Polish priest, son?" Conrad shot the doctor a resentful look.

"I don't know about yours," I swallowed saliva, "but mine doesn't let me sleep at night. He's obsessed with Hitler."

"Hitler!" The writer got up from his chair. "The worthy successor of Leopold!" He shook his head with impatience. "What was it that I said? Ah, that the belief in a supernatural source of evil is not necessary; men alone are quite capable of every wickedness."

"Some men are not even capable of writing in their mother tongue." The doctor regarded us with her impassive eyes. "They would rather fly towards the depths of oblivion."

"Even if man has taken to flying," Conrad went over to the fireplace, "he doesn't fly like an eagle; he flies like a beetle."

"As far as I know, beetles don't write in foreign languages. They lead normal lives."

The writer stroked his beard.

"Is writing not living, *madame*? An artist is a man of action."

"Who instead of acting in his mother tongue betrays her." The doctor made a note in her notebook.

"Ah, from the ship!" Conrad regarded the psychiatrist with serene eyes. "I've been told that I betrayed my language and fatherland in pursuit of popularity."

I burst into tears.

"It was never a matter of choice." The writer put on his cap and stared at the fireplace. "English is not my adopted language. She adopted me."

The doctor regarded us with her impassive eyes.

"The language of solitary hours, of books read," Conrad said in a soft voice but suddenly thundered "Ah, from the ship!" and embraced me again.

"What will happen when we have forgotten the languages we write in?" I sobbed, and Conrad let me go and looked out the window for a few moments.

"I don't know, son. If I had not written in English I would not have written at all."

I swallowed saliva and murmured that I was afraid of not being able to keep writing my novel due to my foreign accent in Antarctic, a language that in the asylum was headed, on a Bartlebian flight, for the depths of oblivion.

"Try to talk about precipices in some other way, son," Conrad gave me a fatherly kiss on the forehead, "and don't worry about your accent. I learned English at twenty, and it was my fourth language after Polish, Russian, and French."

The doctor made a note in her notebook.

"The native English writers said I made the English language anew. And I speak it with a dreadful Polish accent!"

Conrad smiled at the psychiatrist, picked up my glass, drank the water in one gulp, spat it on the floor, and hurled the glass against the wall.

"Ah from the ship! Jettison the cargo that is the mother tongue," and with that he was gone.

The aide gave me an injection, accompanied me to my room, and put me to bed while Father Kalinowski invoked Saint Sebastian, and I pulled the covers over my head and fell asleep. I woke when the priest slapped me several times and said he knew I couldn't sleep and he couldn't sleep either, because he was thinking about a dead bird. I asked if he had tried praying to calm down, and Father Kalinowski sighed and answered that not only had the spot where his canary died been close to a concentration camp and the radio tower where World War II began, but it was also in a mining region where other canaries had been exterminated. Before ventilation systems existed in the mines, the miners took the exotic birds deep underground, for a canary's death was a warning signal that helped them detect a lethal concentration of gases.

I responded that this happened to everyone, as hyperactive Hitler had exterminated many people, but could he please try to use his head over his heart and sleep, for a tough day awaited us. Then I asked if the death of his canary had anything to do with his admission into the Liège psychiatric hospital, but Father Kalinowski got up from the floor, said that he was in the asylum on account of the poultry farming sector, and went back to bed. I lay awake a long time trying to work out what event in my past might have been the warning signal for the current failed state of my sex life, but before I could grow too distressed I fell asleep.

10

I DREAMED that Hitler, a stunt double in an action film, was curled up in the backseat of a car that was careening over a precipice and that his silver Mercedes smashed onto the ground, stirring up a cloud of dust. I woke to a silent room, and when I opened my eyes Father Kalinowski was seated at the table, staring at a spot on the wall. I asked if he'd been to his session with the doctor, but the priest didn't answer, looked at me with absent eyes, hid his face in his hands, and burst into tears. I told him he had to do more sport and hopped onto the stationary bicycle to lead by example, but the vision of my flaccid legs in motion only increased his desolation.

I left the room and went into the doctor's office, where a thunderous shout in an unidentifiable language carried from the treatment room while the psychiatrist consulted her notes. I sat down and, when the psychiatrist asked where I went after visiting the grave of Adolf Hittler in Bucharest, I swallowed saliva and answered, "Nowhere." Awaiting me outside the Jewish cemetery were several native Polish writers who were in the Romanian capital for an international congress, and they gave me a hiding for not writing in my mother tongue. I regained consciousness in the backseat of a black Volga in a parking lot somewhere in Hungary and, when I asked where they were taking me, the Polish intellectuals sprayed my face with tear gas and pulled a paper bag over my head.

Two days later we arrived in Paris and the native Polish writers took me to the Montmartre Cemetery, where, in the Avenue des Polonais, some nineteenth-century military and political Polish personages are buried. The illustrious men of letters threw me to the ground, flattened me against the gravestone of a Romantic poet, thrashed me with their passports, and told me that they were sick to death of my lack of literary patriotism. Then they made me visit the graves of the Polish generals, captains, and counts who were buried in the cemetery and asked me if I understood that patriotism meant not only killing and being killed for the fatherland, but writing in one's mother tongue too. I tried to explain that people such as Bernard Shaw believed that patriotism is one's conviction that one's country is superior to all others because one was born in it, but the Polish intellectuals smacked me with their essays. With that, they threw me to the ground, hit my head against the gravestone of a capo several times, said that this Shaw was a failure, and dragged me by my hair out of the cemetery. I tried to argue that Shaw also believed that we would never have a quiet world till we knocked the patriotism out of the human race, but the native Polish writers dealt me a few final kicks and with that they were gone.

The doctor was making a note in her notebook when a cry carried from the corridor, followed by the sound of a slap and a "Don't touch me, vermin!"; then, the door was kicked open, and into the office came a woman wearing a cloche hat.

"Return to your room, Mrs. Blixen," the doctor regarded the writer with her impassive eyes.

"Baroness Blixen, darling." The woman sat at the desk, crossed her legs, and smiled at me. "You must be the poor specimen from Eastern Europe. Are you still writing your novel in Antarctic?"

I nodded and burst into tears.

"Calm down, darling." The writer patted me on the back. "If you cry they'll think we'll stop writing."

"Would you like to keep writing books in English, Baroness?" The doctor emphasized the final word.

Karen Blixen laughed.

"If it takes my fancy, then of course. What language should I write them in?"

"In your mother tongue, Danish, Baroness Blixen. Like everyone else."

"Do you mean for me to do the same as everyone else, darling?"

The doctor made a note in her notebook.

"Are you trying to convince me that you write in English because it takes your fancy?"

"No," answered the baroness, "I write in English because it's more profitable."

The doctor regarded the writer with her impassive eyes, and Karen Blixen made a bored face.

"Bartlebian therapy this, linguistic reinsertion that, it's always the same bourgeois story. How about you tell me, darling, what your book's about instead?"

"It's about a Polish stunt double who leaps into the void by day, standing in for lead actors during action-film shootings, and writes a novel in an astronomical observatory by night." I looked at the floor.

"Don't worry." Karen Blixen patted me on the back

again. "We all start out with something pretentious."

I sobbed and asked how she avoided getting anxious with Bartlebian therapy.

"I'm very used to these kinds of things." The writer made an elegant gesture of disdain. "If you're a woman you get used to it, because everything you do annoys them. Traveling solo to far-off countries, not wanting a man as a protector guiding you through life, being clever, not writing in your mother tongue. It's dizzying!"

Karen Blixen smiled at the doctor and got up from the desk.

"Why don't you let us write in peace, darling?"

"Do you mean for everyone to do as they wish, Baroness? For everyone to write in a foreign tongue?" The doctor regarded the writer with her impassive eyes.

The writer yawned.

"Literary anarchy, is that what you want?" continued the doctor. "And where would each writer's fatherland be, exactly? How would books be classified in the libraries?"

My nerves betrayed me a little, and I ran over to the bookshelf lined with diagnostic manuals and pulled it over.

"Calm down, darling." Karen Blixen went over to the doctor and patted her on the back. "You don't mean to intimidate someone who fought a lion, do you?"

The psychiatrist made a note in her notebook.

"What's all this fuss about Bartlebian therapy?" The writer smiled. "We must make our mark on life while we have it in our power. What does it matter which language we make it in, darling?"

The doctor didn't answer, and Karen Blixen made a gesture of impatience.

"I have to go, darling. Keep calm, okay? Write a little each day, without hope, without despair. But remember: no protector men and no mother tongues."

Back in my room, silence reigned, as Father Kalinowski was lying with his face to the wall and, contrary to custom, did not even get up to listen to the evening mass on the radio. I made the most of the silence to work on *Kaskader* until late and when I got into bed Ernest came to mind, followed by the Polish writer Stanisław Ignacy Witkiewicz, with whom I never did grow close, for on learning that Stalin had invaded Poland he decided to take his own life. After his suicide I spent months listening to Maria Callas perform *Casta Diva*, reading Descartes, and assuming that doubt was the only certainty when it came to any future erotic activity. From Father Kalinowski's bed came the sounds of heavy breathing, and I switched off the light, imagined a decomposing veterinarian closing a book and sinking his fangs in my faint-hearted neck, and fell asleep.

I woke to someone splashing water on my face and when I opened my eyes it was still night time and Father Kalinowski had sat down on the floor and was hiding his face in his hands. I feigned a few snores, but the priest sighed and said he knew I wasn't sleeping and he couldn't sleep either because he was thinking about a dead bird. I responded that I was sure his canary was much happier up in birdie heaven, but when the priest babbled something about Hitler, my nerves betrayed me a little. I got out of bed, switched on the light, and said that for months I'd slept poorly because of him and that I was fed up with having to deal with his personal problems. Father Kalinowski tried to bless me, but I yanked off my nightshirt and said I wasn't about to listen to another story about dead birds in the wee hours. The priest looked away and said that this time it would be different, but I shrieked that as a would-be veterinarian I forbade him from spouting any more stories about deceased birds, switched off the light, pulled the covers over my head, and fell asleep.

11

I DREAMED that Father Kalinowski's canary caught a cattle wagon from Poland, passed through a Europe in ruins, and arrived in Paris, where the native Antarctic and Polish writers pecked it to death for its exotic plumage. In the morning I was woken by a choked weeping and, when I opened my eyes, the stationary bicycle was unoccupied and Father Kalinowski was still lying with his face to the wall. I sat on his bed and said that he should have listened when I spoke of the importance of rest, and the priest turned over, hugged me, and babbled something about a chicken. When he started howling like an abandoned dog I slapped him twice and said to tell me what was wrong or else I would report him for sexual harassment. Father Kalinowski crossed himself, sat up with difficulty, asked if we could sit at the table, gave a deep sigh, and looked towards the window. Then he crossed himself again and said that the day they committed him to the Liège psychiatric hospital, the police had found him roaming the streets of Spa. The inhabitants of that Belgian village alerted the police to the fact that a foreign priest was wandering around with a plastic bag that had the body of a headless chicken dangling from it. The chicken was Zdzisław, named in honor of a Polish interwar skier, and had led a peaceful life in the allotment garden until Father Kalinowski killed it.

One morning, fed up with the way the chicken regarded him with its indifferent eyes each time he gave it food,

Father Kalinowski left the bowl of wheat on the ground, grabbed an axe, and cut off Zdzisław's head. Appalled by what he had just done, he picked up the chicken head, the crossed eyes of which communicated the dramatic inexpressiveness of one who has seen the hour of one's violent death arrive, and buried it among the beets. Then he tucked the trunk of what had been an apathetic fowl and was now a piece of warm meat into a plastic bag, rode a bike to the station, and caught the first train that went by. When changing trains, he boarded one headed for Germany where a cousin of his lived, but he nodded off, and the train ended up depositing him in the desolate streets of a Belgian village.

Father Kalinowski looked towards the window and said that in the Liège psychiatric hospital he had come to understand that the murder of his canary, perpetrated by the xenophobic sparrows, was just the tip of the iceberg of the animal drama that had not let him get a wink of shuteye for years. He himself killed the chicken Zdzisław because of something that had happened one December night deep in the Communist period when the priest, who at that stage was still a seminarian, had gone to a friend's place to bid him farewell. His friend, who lived with his wife and a sausage dog in the same block of flats, was emigrating in secret to Western Germany the next morning. The future priest arrived home late and, with a few glasses of vodka under his belt, he went into the bathroom and got into the bathtub where three carp were swimming around in the cold water. The presence of those robust fresh-water fish in sanitation facilities had a profound logic in Communist Poland, for during the years when essential items were scarce it was vital to keep the ingredients of the most important Christmas dish alive. Addled by the national alcohol, and engulfed in his contemplations of the sausage dog's future life in the West, Father Kalinowski stayed in the bathtub a long while. When he started to get cold he acted like an unwitting explorer of domestic ecosystems for, without registering a thing, he carried out the necessary hygienic tasks, switched off the light, and went to bed. The next morning, which was the 24th of December, he discovered that he was more alone than ever, not only because his friend's Trabant was no longer parked in front of the block of flats, but also because the protagonists of his Christmas Eve dinner had greeted daybreak floating on their backs.

"Years later," Father Kalinowski kept looking towards the window, "that day in my allotment garden, I cut off the head of a chicken by the name of Zdzisław because it seemed like a just revenge for those carps. And not only for the three I killed without meaning to because I was drunk. For all the carps, each and every one of those vertebrate heroes that, during the long years of Communism, swam around in the dark in Polish bathtubs only to be sacrificed on the altar of the planned economy."

Father Kalinowski hid his face in his hands and stayed seated at the table while I dressed, attempted to bless him, and left for my therapeutic session with the doctor. The hospital was silent, and when I went into the psychiatrist's office I saw an elderly man sitting in the chair before the desk, his chin resting in his hand, looking at me with a weary expression.

"Now it's your fellow countryman's turn," the doctor regarded him with her impassive eyes. "We're almost done, Mr. Ionesco."

"My countryman?" The man got up, came over to the door, and held out his hand. "Eugène Ionesco," he sat down again and turned his dull gaze on the doctor.

"Don't look at me like that. You're both from Eastern Europe."

I leaned against the doorframe and looked at the floor.

"We've spoken about this many times, Doctor," answered Ionesco in a mild tone. "I'm French. A French writer."

"Of course." The doctor made a note in her notebook. "You're a French writer. And why is it that you have a Romanian surname?"

I sobbed from the doorway, and Ionesco placated me with a gesture.

"You would have to ask my parents, Doctor," he responded politely before sighing and looked towards the office window. "You know my story. My father was Romanian and my mother, French. We arrived in France when I was one."

"Of course." The doctor regarded him with her impassive eyes. "And you never went home to Romania, correct? You lived all your life in France?"

"No," answered Ionesco in a weary voice. "Yes." For a moment it was as if he were going to get up but, in the end, he didn't move from the chair. "I've told you several times, Doctor. We left France when I was thirteen years old."

The doctor made a note in her notebook and Eugène

Ionesco looked at me, dejected.

"Are you Prześnicki?"

I nodded and swallowed saliva.

"Have you also..." Ionesco searched for words. "Do they also make you..."

"Every time I come here," I murmured and sobbed, and the doctor regarded me with her impassive eyes.

From the treatment room came a shout, and Ionesco glanced at the doctor with a resigned look on his face.

"May I leave?"

"Not before explaining the French writer thing."

"Ah, yes." Ionesco made a fatalistic wave of his hand and leaned forward in his chair. "I'll explain it to you once more, Doctor. I'm French. I learned my language as an infant."

The doctor made a note in her notebook.

"And your mother tongue?"

I emitted a choked weeping, leaned more heavily against the doorframe, and slid down it until I was sitting on the floor.

"I just explained it to you, Doctor," continued Ionesco with perfect patience. "I learned French when I was little."

"French." The doctor regarded him with her impassive eyes. "And your mother tongue? Romanian, Mr. Ionesco?"

I whimpered, and Ionesco raised his eyebrows, rocked back in his chair, and looked at the ceiling. Then he pursed his lips, rested the front legs of the chair on the floor again, and repeated his words in a mild tone once more.

"Doctor. I had to travel to Romania with my father, when I was thirteen. Remember that. I learned Romanian in Bucharest. Each time we see each other I have to repeat the same thing."

"That's because each time we see each other you tell me the same thing." The doctor was making a note in her notebook.

"What do you want me to say?" Ionesco looked at her with a weary expression. "When we left France, my world was shattered."

"When you and your family left for Eastern Europe." The doctor regarded him with her impassive eyes.

"For Eastern Europe," Ionesco repeated robotically and observed with dismay my difficulties breathing.

"Are you from Poland?" he asked.

"Yes," I responded in a choked voice, "I'm from Poland."

"From Eastern Europe." The doctor regarded me with her impassive eyes.

"Yes," I responded. "From Eastern Europe." And then my nerves betrayed me a little, I got up off the floor, went over to the desk, and pounded it with my fists. "Yes, Doctor! From Eastern Europe!"

I remained like that for a few seconds, catching my breath, and then bellowed:

"From Eastern Europe! Where white bears wander the streets! Where it's always cold and we while away the day eating pork fat and drinking vodka!"

The doctor made a note in her notebook, and Ionesco sighed and looked towards the window.

"Eastern Europe!" I gasped, pounding the desk.

"Where mustachioed men wander about, clutching plastic bags and prattling in Russian about the wars and communism!"

"Well they do wander about, don't they?" The doctor regarded me with her impassive eyes.

Ionesco looked at me, his expression weary.

"Wander," he repeated robotically. "Wandering. The story of my life is the story of a wandering."

I sobbed, kicked the doctor's chair, and fell to the floor, and the psychiatrist made a note in her notebook.

"Such as when you travelled to France once more?" she asked, and Ionesco opened his mouth to respond but closed it again because the doctor went on, "Why did you leave Romania? Didn't you like your country?"

"My country," repeated Ionesco before adding in a mild tone, "I had already lost my country, Doctor. France was my childhood paradise. I was inconsolable."

From the treatment room came a shout in an unidentifiable language.

"The children laughed at my accent when I spoke Romanian. You and I talked about this, remember. I pronounced my r's as the French do and this meant I not only sounded foreign; I sounded like a Jew."

Ionesco looked towards the window.

"Like a Jew," he repeated and looked at me. "Can I leave now, Doctor?"

I whimpered from the floor.

"Not until you give me an answer, Mr. Ionesco. Why did you travel to France?" The doctor regarded him with her impassive eyes.

"Travel to France," Ionesco repeated robotically and

looked at the doctor, his expression weary. "I planned to go home right away. As soon as I could. Remember that, Doctor. But first, I had to get through school and university. And secure a grant."

The doctor made a note in her notebook.

"Why do you make a note of everything?" Ionesco asked in a mild tone. "I've told you all this so many times."

"In the end, you managed to travel to France." The doctor didn't look up from the notebook.

"In the end, I managed to go home to France." There was dismay in Ionesco's big eyes. "With a doctoral grant, fifteen years later. I took fifteen years to go home to my country. To go home once and for all." He sighed and looked towards the window. "You know how it went, Doctor. We talk about this each time I come here."

"We also talk about your Romanian surname." The doctor regarded him with her impassive eyes.

Ionesco brushed his forehead with his hand and looked at me, tired.

"You also... You..."

I nodded and hiccupped from the floor, and Ionesco got up, bent over, and looked at me closely with his big eyes.

"I've heard you're writing a book in Antarctic, Prześnicki," he said in a mild tone. "What about? Eastern Europe?"

"Not about Eastern Europe at all," I sobbed, getting to my feet with difficulty, "but about a Polish stunt double who leaps into the void by day and writes a novel in an astronomical observatory by night."

"Leaps into the void," Ionesco repeated robotically

and made a resigned gesture with his hand.

The doctor made a note in her notebook:

"Prześnicki doesn't write in his mother tongue either, Mr. Ionesco."

"But I do write in my mother tongue, Doctor, remember that."

The doctor regarded us with her impassive eyes.

"Do you think I'll forget Antarctic?" I whimpered and clutched Ionesco by the elbow, but he only looked at me in dismay. "Why are you classified time and again as a Romanian writer," I burst into tears and clutched him harder, "when you learned Romanian at thirteen and wrote in French all your life?"

Ionesco sighed, tried without success to free himself, and looked with resignation towards the office door.

"Is it because you have a foreign surname?"

"Can I go, Doctor?" Ionesco looked at the psychiatrist.

"Do you think they know better? Do you think they're best placed to know what our mother tongue is?" I sobbed, and the doctor regarded us with her impassive eyes and made a note in her notebook. "Do you think they need to assign us a concrete culture?" I kept on, now short of breath. "A clear origin? A particular language?" I let go of Ionesco's elbow and sank my hands into my thinning hair. "Do you think that by making us fit into a rigid order, they order their own world?"

Ionesco pursed his lips and looked at me, his expression weary.

"Why do people expect authors to answer questions?" He opened the door. "I'm an author because I want to ask questions. If I had answers, I would be a politician."

Ionesco departed the office, and the doctor ignored a desperate shout that was coming from the treatment room, ordered me to sit, consulted her notes, and asked what happened after the native Polish writers left me in the Montmartre Cemetery.

I responded that I went to the Antarctic Embassy in Paris to seek political asylum on the grounds of literary persecution, but in the foyer I came across the native Antarctic writers, who were in the French capital for a tribute to their illustrious careers. The sage intellectuals donged me with the medals they had just been awarded and asked why we miserable immigrants were never satisfied working in intercultural mediation or for one of the not-for-profits that promoted dialogue with our countries. Then they tied me up, stuffed me into the boot of a Ford Fiesta, and three hours later pulled me out of the car in the region of Belgium that during World War I was known by the name of Ypres Salient. There the native Antarctic writers dragged me to one of the Commonwealth cemeteries, tied me to the grave of a soldier from the Māori Pioneer Battalion who died on New Year's Eve of 1917, and told me this was what happened to those who ventured too far from their home countries. After the sage men of letters dealt me a few final kicks and departed, I got up, went around looking at the rest of the cemetery graves, and, when I read on one of them the epitaph "Sacrificed to a fallacy," I remembered my novel *Wampir* and burst into tears. Then I walked to the main road and hitchhiked to nearby Bayernwald, where hyperactive Hitler served as a message runner three years before the New Zealand soldiers set out across the world, destined for a trench in the north of Europe.

The doctor made a note in her notebook, and I asked if she was familiar with the photograph of young Hitler in Bayernwald, taken in 1914, in which the future chancellor of the Third Reich appears alongside other military men and a little white dog. The dog rests its front paws on the knees of one of the other soldiers but stretches its snout towards the last man in the row, Hitler, who directs his tormented gaze at the photographer. The doctor asked if I thought that dog had served in World War I, and I responded that in World War I not only dogs served, but horses, messenger pigeons, and the odd bear did too. Then I swallowed saliva and said that the Bayernwald dog seemed to sense that the man who said that the more he knew people, the more he loved his dog Blondi, would go far.

The fire had gone out, and I added that in the Bayernwald trenches there not only lived a dog but also a canary that escaped from the Australian diggers. The Ypres front moved very little, for the two sides were in trenches facing each other, unable to advance any further, so the allies decided to dig tunnels to blow up the German positions. The diggers worked in secret with the intention of surprising the enemy until the day that one of the canaries they utilized to detect poisonous gases escaped, flew to the surface, and perched a few meters from the trench. Unaware that it was putting the whole operation in danger, for a canary in a Belgian wood was clear proof of the existence of a tunnel, the bird started preening itself. When the snipers that aimed at it missed and their shots alerted the soldiers in the trench facing them, the canary met its fate by way of a lobbed grenade.

The doctor made a note in her notebook, and I said that Hitler returned to Bayernwald at the beginning of June in 1940, a few days before the fall of Paris and soon before the first cattle wagon of prisoners arrived at the Auschwitz concentration camp. The chancellor of the Third Reich would get out of the car and make for the wood that had inspired him to paint his artwork *Croonaert* and where years before he had won the Iron Cross. On leaving a small clearing he would remember the white dog and, following a strange urge, would keep walking among the trees until he arrived at the spot where the grenade had exploded. There he would crouch, gaze in dread at a hat with a yellow feather, feel faint, goose step back to the silver Mercedes, and shout at the driver to step on it. He would huddle in the backseat and hold his breath until the car had carried him far from the explosion that twenty-six years before had transmitted via radiofrequency a warning signal from the future.

The aide gave me an injection, and when I went back to my room Father Kalinowski, who had prostrated himself in the form of a cross before the photo of Karol Wojtyła, got to his feet, sighed, and left for his session with the doctor. I started writing on the old pages of *De Standaard*, and when tears started springing from my eyes because I couldn't remember how to end several figures of speech in Antarctic, the priest returned and said that the doctor had discharged him. He packed his suitcase, sat on my bed, handed over his headlamp, gave me a heavy-hearted look, and said he was positive that one of these days I would stop practicing sex with other men and would start a family.

"But the problem is that I don't practice sex with other men, Father." I burst into tears.

Father Kalinowski blessed me and got to his feet.

"Does it truly not bother you, not having a sex life?" I sobbed. "And do you think there will be restitution for those carp?"

The priest picked up his suitcase from the floor.

"Don't you ever feel like reading a little philosophy, Father?"

"Philosophers are dangerous."

"I don't know what to say to you," my nerves betrayed me a little. "The philosopher has never killed any priest, whereas the priest has killed a great many philosophers."

Father Kalinowski smiled and traced the sign of a cross on the spot where my thinning hair began.

"Denis Diderot said it." I swallowed saliva.

The priest opened the door.

"May God bless you, Czesław."

12

I DREAMED I was lining up to buy toilet paper alongside an Enlightenment philosopher and when I woke
in my room it was cold, Father Kalinowski's bed wasn't
unmade, and from the wall a smiling Karol Wojtyła was
gazing down at me. I went to the doctor's office, and the
psychiatrist ignored some stifled shrieks in an unidentifiable language and asked what happened in Bayernwald to
result in a Belgian police patrol coming across me wandering around the city of Liège. I failed to answer, and
the doctor pulled out of the drawer a crinkled paper, on
which someone had written in uppercase I GOT MY START
WITH RUNOVER DOGS, and placed it on the desk. Then
she regarded me with her impassive eyes, said that when
the ambulance brought me to the asylum I had this note
in my hand, and asked me why I had written it and when
I intended to devote myself finally to veterinary sciences.

I answered that the phrase was not mine but the Belgian writer Georges Simenon's and explained that it was
his means of describing in French his beginnings as a
reporter, when he was filing human interest stories for
the local paper *La Gazette de Liège*. The doctor made a
note in her notebook, and I said that, when I saw that no
one was awaiting me outside Bayernwald, I went on foot
to the nearest train station and hopped onto the first
train that pulled in. When the train took off, the driver
announced through the loudspeaker that the train was
headed for Liège, and I understood that finding myself

en route to the city where Simenon had started writing couldn't have been a coincidence. I remembered his phrase and jotted it down on a piece of paper I found on the seat, which was as much out of solidarity with Rex, the dogged detective, as it was in the hope of following in the footsteps of a writer who not only became a master of style and wrote more than two hundred novels, but also declared that he had made love to ten thousand women.

From the treatment room came a protracted wail, and the doctor asked what some runover dogs from the early twentieth century had to do with the fact that the police found me stark naked in the Outremeuse neighborhood. I took a nervous sip of water and answered that when I arrived in Liège, I followed in Simenon's footsteps all over the city and got most excited not outside the house where he was born, occupied now by the African hairdressing salon known as George, but on the Pont des Arches. This bridge was where Simenon's first novel began, and I stayed a long while leaning on the rail, gazing down at the Meuse River, and thinking about the failure of my first novel, *Wampir*. An elderly gentleman passed by, accompanied by an old mid-sized dog with red fur, an unsteady step, and eyes covered in a thin white film that indicated advanced cataracts. I turned my head, saw how the dog and its master moved away, and thought about Simenon, who said that a writer is no prize cow to hang with medals and that one must experience, feel, have boxed, and have lied, not in depth, but enough to understand. When I arrived at the conclusion that the failure of my first novel must have been due to my scant experience as a boxer, the blind dog tripped at a gap in the pavement and banged clumsily against the rail, and then its little body traced a perfect arc from the Pont des Arches to where it plunged into the Meuse. A few seconds later it broke the surface and started paddling its front paws, desperate, and I remembered a Goya painting, thought that since I didn't know how to operate on the blind dog's cataracts the least I could do was save its life, scrambled up onto the rail, and leaped.

The doctor regarded me with her impassive eyes, and I said that when I managed to get my head above water I saw the blind dog walking, dripping wet, along the pavement that skirted the river, its step calm and a large rock in its muzzle. I emerged from the Meuse several hundred meters downriver, stripped off my soaking-wet clothes, and started walking in circles around a bench, where a few hours later I was picked up by a Belgian bicycle patrol. The police officers called an ambulance, and although the driver complained about the number of patients that the health sector of a country that had had no government for the past year needed to process, he took me to the Liège psychiatric hospital.

The doctor was making a note in her notebook when the door opened and in came a bespectacled woman who went over to the bookshelf lined with diagnostic manuals and pulled it over with such force that I burst into tears.

"Ionesco told me you were a little sensitive." The woman took a pack of cigarettes out of her pocket and lit one.

"Prześnicki, isn't it?" She took a deep drag.

"Out for a stroll, Mrs. Kristof?" The doctor regarded

the writer with her impassive eyes.

My nerves betrayed me a little and I prostrated myself in the form of a cross before Agota Kristof, said I'd read all her books, sobbed, and asked if her French was likewise headed, on a Bartlebian flight, for the depths of oblivion.

"You think too much, Przęśnicki." Agota Kristof took another drag of her cigarette. "What you need is to stop daydreaming about abysses and to concentrate on your novel."

"Giving out free advice, Mrs. Kristof?" The doctor made a note in her notebook. "Didn't you say that French was an enemy language because it made you illiterate and almost killed your Hungarian?"

"You've almost killed my Antarctic," I sobbed from the floor.

"Not having chosen to write in a foreign language." The doctor regarded me with her impassive eyes.

"I did not choose French," Agota Kristof exhaled smoke in the doctor's direction, "It was imposed upon me by fate, by chance, by circumstance."

"Well, these days fate, chance, or circumstance is imposing Bartlebian therapy upon you." The doctor made a note in her notebook.

I burst into tears.

"You think too much about Bartlebian therapy, Przęśnicki." Agota Kristof tapped the ash from her cigarette onto the doctor's desk. "I have spoken French for more than thirty years, I have written French for twenty years, but I still don't know it. I don't speak it without mistakes, and I can only write it with the help of dictionaries, which I frequently consult."

"Soon you won't need even the dictionary," the doctor examined the ash up close, "because you will have forgotten it entirely."

"The important thing, Prześnicki," Agota Kristof took a quick drag of her cigarette, "is writing. First you have to write. Then you have to keep writing. Even if what you write is of no interest to anyone."

"It is certainly of interest to us," the doctor made a note in her notebook, "because you are taking advantage of a country that has had no government for the past year."

The writer exhaled smoke towards the ceiling.

"Even if you believe that what you write will never be of interest to anyone."

"My novel *Wampir* has never been of interest to anyone," I sobbed. "Only to the native Antarctic writers."

"You think too much about those people, Prześnicki." Agota Kristof stubbed out the cigarette on the doctor's desk. "I know I will never write in French as native French writers do, but I will write it as I am able to, as best I can."

My nerves betrayed me a little, I got up and ran over to the bookshelf lined with diagnostic manuals, but on seeing it was already on the floor I sobbed and sank my hands into my thinning hair.

"And what if we never leave the asylum? What if we forget the languages we write in?"

"You think too much, Prześnicki." Agota Kristof flicked the butt towards the fireplace. "I would have written anywhere. In any language."

The writer lit another cigarette and left, and the doctor made a note in her notebook, gazed at the smear of ash, opened the desk drawer, and retrieved a few old pages of *De Standaard*. Then she regarded me with her impassive eyes and said that, before departing, Father Kalinowski had expressed concerns about my moral state and had given her my novel, which he had found ensconced in the bathroom. The doctor added that I should be grateful to the staff at the Liège psychiatric hospital for their ongoing efforts to improve the mental and physical wellbeing of my faint-hearted self. They had tolerated my continued insistence on writing in Antarctic because, according to Bartlebian therapy treatment protocols, the healing process is sped up when the patient has an illusion of freedom. But now that the treatment was about to conclude, there was no justification for my chronic squandering of paper, especially when the country to which the paper belonged had had no government for the past year.

The doctor got up, took hold of the old pages of *De Standaard*, went over to the fireplace, threw my novel into the flames, and said that my Antarctic had just headed, on a Bartlebian flight, for the depths of oblivion. Afterwards she opened the office door, and my nerves betrayed me a little, for I howled like an abandoned dog, jumped onto her back, and sank my fangs into her impassive neck.

The aides straitjacketed me, carted me off to the treatment room, tied my hands and feet to a metal table, switched off the light, closed the door, and departed. For a few seconds the room remained in silence and then I heard a metallic noise, and *Casta Diva*, in a performance by Danuta Lato, started playing through the loudspeaker. I lost all sense of time and I'm not sure how long it was before the singer choked and went quiet and someone came into the room and started touching my privates. As I was starting to get aroused the light came on, and the aide who was untying me told me to stop shouting because the days of having an injections budget were over. He added that everything was over, for the doctor, who had taken advantage of the lack of government to implement therapies of personal interest, had just eloped to Veracruz with Doctor Pasavento.

I got down from the table, burst into tears, and asked what the rest of the staff of the Liège psychiatric hospital intended to do with us.

"Here in Belgium we haven't had a government for the past year, Przęśnicki." The aide regarded me with his impassive eyes. "Do you suppose we have nothing better to do than waste our time on foreign writers?"

I left the treatment room and heard voices coming from the doctor's office, and when I opened the door the rest of the hospital patients greeted me with applause, hugs, and a punch here and there. Together we smashed the psychiatrist's desk, tossed the chairs out the window, and drank three bottles of champagne that Nabokov found in the medicine cabinet. We were burning the doctor's diagnostic manuals in the fireplace when a knock at the door sounded and a bearded man in a thick coat came into the office.

"Men wanted for hazardous journey!" he bellowed from beneath his fur hat.

No one said a word.

"Small wages! Bitter cold! Long months of complete darkness! Constant danger! Safe return doubtful!" The man removed his hat. "Honor and recognition in case of success!"

Joseph Conrad spat champagne onto the floor, and my nerves betrayed me a little as I asked the bearded man who he was.

"I'm Shackleton, the polar explorer." The man unbuckled his jacket. "I'm looking for volunteers to journey to Antarctica."

Conrad elbowed me, and I swallowed saliva and murmured that I would like to go but I couldn't return to the very place I'd been ousted from.

"Who ousted you from Antarctica?" Shackleton shrugged off his coat.

"The native Antarctic writers." I looked at the floor, remembered *Wampir* and *Kaskader*, and burst into tears.

"Writers, they had to be writers." Shackleton wiped sweat from his brow. "It's because the ecosystem was disturbed and the predators quickly multiplied. But now they are under control."

"What do you mean?" I sobbed. "Are there no native Antarctic writers left in Antarctica?"

"There are indeed, but almost all of them are in a reservation." Shackleton went over to the window and glanced at the street. "We pacify the two who remain on the loose with a medal a day. We had to shut away the others, they were aggressive and kept attacking indigenous species. That's why we need so many veterinarians. Someone's got to supervise the repopulation of the emperor penguin."

The polar explorer slipped his coat back on.

"If no one is interested, then I have to go because my dogs are outside."

"Dogs?"

"Sixty-nine dogs, yes, sir." There was a note of impatience in Shackleton's voice. "And we are keen to be off because of the heat."

Surrounding the sled parked out the front of the Liège psychiatric hospital was a happy multitude of honest quadrupeds of assorted fur and powerful paws and with mischievous twinkles in their eyes, and on seeing us they proceeded to jump up and down, bark, and lick any exposed skin.

Shackleton took up the reins of the sled.

"Ready to travel to Antarctica?"

"Yes, Mr. Shackleton." I pulled on his fur hat.

The polar explorer winked at me.

"Call me Ernest."

13

Antarctic Writers' Association
Vinson
Antarctica

Czesław Przęśnicki
En route to Antarctica

Dear Mr. Przęśnicki:

Regarding: Invitation

Please accept this letter as notification
that at the Annual General Meeting of the
Antarctic Writers' Association (hereinafter "the Association"), held on the
15th of the current month on the
Vinson reservation, a motion was passed,
in keeping with the Association's remit
and statutory goals, to formulate the
observations communicated herein.

The Association declares the following:

Czesław Przęśnicki (hereinafter "the
aspirant"), citizen of Eastern Europe and
resident of Antarctica (residency type
and duration: lapsed temporary authori-
zation), current address unknown, is the

author of the work *Wampir* (language and
territory: Antarctica; publication sta-
tus: remaindered).

The Association's statutory goals include
intercultural dialogue, with special em-
phasis on dialogue with immigrants, which
is accomplished through a range of activities to promote gastronomy, folklore,
music, and other aspects of the cultures
from which these individuals originate.

The Association acknowledges and regrets
the injuries, none of which were of a permanent nature, incurred upon the aspirant
under the influence of alcohol ingested by
mistake, the infliction of such injuries
conflicting as it does with the Association's scope of activity, the purpose
of which is to protect and shelter immigrants in their natural ignorance of the
laws, customs, and language of the host
country.

The Association has determined the
following:

In recognition of the above, and taking
into account that the aspirant fulfils the
prerequisites for the election of office-
bearers, the Association, in a move

towards restitution for the damage
caused, and in pursuit of greater di-
versity within its ranks, grants the
aspirant the office of secretary.

Notwithstanding the priority conferred
in the Association's statutes on re-
cruiting natives from the geographical
areas of greatest renown with a view to
boosting the Association's prestige, the
Association, recognizing the unfeasibil-
ity of fulfilling said criterion in the
current socio-economic environment, has
resolved to opt for an Eastern-European
citizen, while stressing that such an ar-
rangement implies less of a drain on the
Association's coffers.

The rights and obligations of secretaries
are stipulated in appendix 1, included
herein, and include performing all clean-
ing, maintenance, and general upkeep of
the Association's establishments; translating the works by both rank-and-file
members and the board of directors and
disseminating said works abroad; and
attending to the telephone.

In order to deliver on its good faith, and
in the spirit of this mutual understand-
ing, the Association commits to funding

any kind of therapeutic support required
by the aspirant, notably concerning be-
havioral issues (see appendix 2, section
3a, "Biting objects and persons"), as well
as obsessive-compulsive behaviors (see
appendix 2, section 3b, "Cemeteries").

In recognition of the aspirant's merit,
observable in the fact that he wrote
the abovementioned *Wampir* in Antarctic,
thereby demonstrating a notable effort
to integrate into the host country, the
Association awards the aspirant a multi-
cultural prize and a permanent residency
permit for Antarctica.

On the 31st of the current month, the
admission of the aspirant into the Association will be celebrated, an occasion
to which he is formally invited after
paying the dues and which, in the event
that he has family or friends, he may attend accompanied by the same, provided
that each person bring a minimum of two
bottles of alcohol representative of
their countries of origin, all of which
will be collected at the entrance for
subsequent cultural analysis.

Having nothing further to add, we remain
sincerely yours,

Antarctic Writers' Association

(signed)

I FELL hard for this erudite, madcap romp of a book. A bookseller in Barcelona pressed it into my hands in February 2016, a few months after it was released by small, prestigious press Editorial Minúscula. "If you want to read something that says this much" – he opened his arms wide – "then this is the book for you." He couldn't have put it better: as you know by now, *The Palimpsests*'s slight dimensions belie how exceptional and ambitious it is.

Fittingly for a piece of writing set in an asylum, working on the translation induced in me a state of low-level paranoia that I can mostly put down to two things. The first was *The Palimpsests*'s bolero effect, its crescendo of repetitions and near repetitions. I had to keep careful track of these, making sure I was translating them the same way, or with the same degree of variation, checking and re-checking as I went, but also rewriting them each time a new context required that I think about how the phrase could fit in this instance while also suiting all the previous ones.

The second was the novel's daisy chain of literary references. These come in the form of quotes that are not signaled as quotes and are sometimes tweaked or reworked (one of the ways that this text is very much the palimpsest). And so, deep inside the translation process, I entered a heightened state of alert, seeing signs where none existed, spending hours chasing a single phantom quote that often turned out not to be a quote at all. My reward? The rush when

---

[1] Many of these references were from English-language texts, but for those

an elusive suspect turned out to be a slight rewording, ensconced in a text that wasn't available online.[1]

Yet by opening with two of this translation's challenges, I don't mean to detract from the rare enchantments of this translation project. *The Palimpsests* is full of incidents that are astonishingly inventive, and never before have I found myself laughing out loud so often while working alone at my desk. Although, "alone" doesn't capture exactly how it felt – I knew that Aleksandra was at her desk too, but on the other side of the world, working on her second novel. The telekinetic sense across distance only deepened when a package landed in the letterbox of my Melbourne rental on Yalukit (Boon Wurrung) land, its postage stamp featuring a bridge and rocky shore, its contents a Għar Dalam postcard and a calendar of black-and-white photographs of writers and their most famous lines. The postcard read, in Spanish, "If you asked me why I'm sending you

that weren't, kudos to the translators before me whose choices I've incorporated here, in this way ensuring a ring of familiarity for readers who know the texts from their English-language incarnations: Stephen Kessler's 2004 translation of Luis Cernuda's "Return to Darkness" in *Written in Water*; Walter Kaufmann's 1974 translation of Nietzsche's *The Gay Science*; Jason Weiss's 1984/1986 translations of his interviews with Emil Cioran for *The Los Angeles Times* and *Grand Street*, Richard Howard's 1991 translation of Cioran's *Anathemas and Admirations*, and Ilinca Zarifopol-Johnston's 1995 translation of Cioran's *Tears and Saints*; Susha Guppy's translation of her interview with Eugène Ionesco for *The Paris Review* in 1984; and Nina Bogin's 2014 translation of Agota Kristoff's *The Illiterate*. (Translations of Lecretius and Denis Diderot were from popular sources; I translated, from Lun's renderings of him in Spanish, Georges Simenon, as well as Nicanor Parra and Witold Gombrowicz).

an Irish calendar from Malta, I wouldn't know how to respond. But I know that you – an Australian translator of a Polish author who writes in Spanish and lives in Belgium – will understand." So it goes without saying, I hope, that recreating the voice of Aleksandra's brilliant invention, Przęśnicki, has been the greatest of joys.

~

I set myself some guidelines for translating the exquisite, peculiar humor of *The Palimpsests*. Przęśnicki's childhood in communist Poland and his ongoing therapy mean that, on a linguistic level, this humor partly resides in his consummate wielding of technocratic language and of psychobabble, so I have made sure to stick to the argot of these realms. For example, as much as I would have liked to translate "acomplejados seguro que sí" as "we certainly had hang-ups," "we certainly had complexes" it is.

Only outside these contexts have I taken more creative liberties. Some examples: "vestido" has a constellation of meanings in Spanish that includes dress, gown, and robes in English; it is of course "robes" when worn by a man, but I think neglecting to evoke the image of a gender-fluid pope would be a lost opportunity, thus "dress" it is. Elsewhere, I have made use of alliteration, metaphor, and animalification, as well as a humorous rhythm, to render "la rigidez capilar y mental de las dependientas" (the shop assistants' capillary and mental rigidity – an allusion to their perms and authoritarian inflexibility) as "the shop assistants' rigidity of mind and mane."

And much of the humor is wrapped up in Lun's impeccable style, which makes use of the relative flexibility of word order that is particular to Spanish. If you could stand a sentence on its head, it would be a stack of blocks, with qualification after qualification adding unexpected details to the noun or noun phrase preceding it. English's reduced syntactical flexibility meant that recreating this style required careful thought, reordering, and occasional acrobatics, including locative and directive inversion, for example, but only when those choices didn't draw too much attention to themselves.

~

Nowadays it goes without saying that every translation has a political dimension. But Lun's pointed commentary on the problems and privileges of artistic creation and reception, especially when these activities are shadowed by nativism, meant I was repeatedly reminded of this while I worked. Of course, if the sage intellectuals of Antarctica had it their way, Pręśnicki and other talented souls who write outside their mother tongue would never write, let alone go on to be translated. Which made my task of translating a debut exophonic writer whose novel is all about exophony feel like an act of defiance. That the translation was happening in English – globally the most insular language of all, going by the enormous amount of literature translated out of it and the comparatively miniscule amount translated into it – seemed downright radical.

There is something of the language-learner perfectionism about Pręśnicki's narrative voice, a fastidiousness to his syntax and grammar that I sought to recreate, as well as a bowerbird-like urge to show off the shiny new words he has foraged (I like to imagine he would be tickled by the specificity of the English verbs "careen," or "thwack," or "jettison," for example).

And polyglossia – the coexistence of two or more languages – is the air that everyone in the Liège psychiatric hospital breathes. Europe is portrayed as a palimpsest, with time strangely flattened and the past inscribed in the present and as a linguistic playground. Przęśnicki and his roommate are Polish; they are in francophone Belgium; Przęśnicki is writing his second novel in Antarctic; he is doing so on the pages of a Belgian Dutch-language newspaper. Presumably, Przęśnicki speaks to his roommate in Polish and to the doctor and fellow exophonic writer-patients in either French or, lingua franca that it has become in Europe, English.

At first, I was tempted to highlight the added layer of polyglossia that the translated version of the work gains, wanting to include textual markers that point to the source language. How playful and disorienting it would be, for example, if the toilet-paper-hoarding *Homo sovieticus* in Poland were addressed as "señorita" instead of "Miss".

But a few things stopped me. In no instance does the dialogue suggest communication in a certain language (hence my "presumably" above). The writers committed to the asylum may have accents, but their speech as represented on the page bears no linguistic trace of them. And Przęśnicki never reflects on the fact that his story is narrated in Spanish, nor is there any internal evidence that points to his knowing that language.

In other words, Spanish is the windowpane readers peer through to see into the lives of Przęśnicki and co., and the transparency of that pane is in many ways the metafictional point: look at the linguistic and literary heights that a non-native writer, Lun, can achieve. We viewers of these people's lives forget we're looking through a windowpane at all, which made me reluctant to draw attention to it. Elements such as the title page, Lun's bio, and the blurb were the places where this work should happen, I ultimately decided, not the text itself.

~

You may have noticed that *The Palimpsests* makes an exception to its no-foreign-terms rule for some newspaper and book titles, among them *Wampir* and *Kaskader*, Przęśnicki's books. His novel titles are not only a rare instance of foreign terms in the otherwise-Spanish-only *Los Palimpsestos*, but they also create linguistic evidence of polyglossia on the novel-within-a-novel level of both of those books, for they make them Antarctic publications with Polish titles. Przęśnicki explains his motivations in one case, and in doing so constructs a translation puzzle for me: he says the word for "double" in Polish – "kaskader" – is "more expressive."

He's making a tri-lingual pun: he has given the Polish word not for the more general "double," which has a larger constellation of meanings, but for "stuntman" or "stunt double." He says that this word is more fitting because of the way it sounds, which he then describes in imagistic terms that together paint a picture of a stunt being performed in a car. A prominent aspect of this stunt image is "helmet" – "casco" in Spanish, which of course recalls the first syllable of the Polish "kaskader." So the peculiar logic of his statement hinges on this instance of word play. How to make it work in English?

After a lot of wrestling with myself, and since "helmet" comes amid other descriptions, including "movement forward," I decided to substitute "helmet" with "a cascade of," i.e.:

SOURCE TEXT:	GLOSS:	FINAL TRANSLATION:
[Kaskader] era una palabra más adecuada porque contenía sonidos rudos e invocaba movimiento hacia delante, casco, frenazo, nube de polvo y salto de un coche que seguía hacia el precipicio.	[Kaskader] was a more appropriate word because it contained crude sounds and invoked movement forward, helmet, braking, cloud of dust, and leap from a car that continued towards the precipice.	[Kaskader] was a more fitting word because its harsh sounds evoked a cascade of forward movement, a screeching of brakes, a cloud of dust, and a leap from a car that kept on towards the precipice.

My early drafts included alliteration of the hard 'c-' sound ("it contained crude sounds that conjured a cascade of"), but on reflection it seemed to me that the alliteration hid, or at least drew attention away from, the pun embedded in "cascade".

~

Another first: the delight of translating work by a writer who is a translator too (albeit a much more accomplished, polyglot one!). Aleksandra had a few requests for me that aligned with her own preferences when writing this text: to ensure the length of each sentence, excluding dialogue, was at least two lines long wherever possible; and to use a bare minimum of adverbs. English is on average more succinct than Spanish, and it doesn't have the same preference for abstract nouns, which meant finding creative solutions for the places where no adverb in Spanish would usually require one in English – in Spanish a Maria Callas song might "resonar con fuerza" (resound with force/forcefully), or Nabokov might look at his boxing glove "con detenimiento" (with care/carefully), for example. In these cases I've made the verbs work harder; thus, the Maria Callas song "is blaring" and Nabokov "inspects" or "examines" his glove. Other solutions required a little more thought: one dog looks at the lady shop assistant with "una mirada pícara" (a mischievous gaze/mischievously), which I render "a mischievous twinkle in its eyes". It has been the greatest fun, and a rare privilege, to geek out together over possible choices, and Aleksandra's faith, encouragement, and generosity throughout the process are impossible to overstate.

Thanks are also due to the Ian Potter Cultural Fund and Copyright Agency for making it possible for me to attend the Bread Loaf Translators' Conference, where I was fortunate to participate in a workshop with the brilliant and inspiring Esther Allen and with other attendees who fast became friends. That workshop has made this a better translation. And being awarded a PEN/Heim Translation Fund Grant the following year meant that I could dedicate the time needed for such a challenging work and still feed myself.

~

Przęśnicki, in the months after Vonnegut writes him a letter, consoles himself by reading Ludwig Wittgenstein. This Austrian philosopher isn't quoted in *The Palimpsests*, but he once said, as reported by his friend Norman Malcom in his 1958 memoir about him, "A serious and good philosophical work could be written consisting entirely of jokes." Lun's novel – through offering backstage access to the phenomena of foreign writers and their decision to switch languages, and through confronting us time and again with the political dimension of artistic creation and reception – is incontrovertible proof of that.

— ELIZABETH BRYER

ABOUT THE AUTHOR

ALEKSANDRA LUN left Poland at 19, financed her studies in languages and literature in Spain by working at a casino, and now lives in Belgium. She translates from English, French, Spanish, Italian, Catalan, and Romanian into Polish, her mother tongue. Among other works, she has translated a book of conversations with Jorge Luis Borges. Her first novel *The Palimpsests*, written in Spanish, has already been published in France, where it garnered critical acclaim, and its translation into English was awarded a PEN/Heim grant from PEN America.

ABOUT THE TRANSLATOR

ELIZABETH BRYER is a translator and writer. In 2017 she was a recipient of a PEN/Heim Translation Fund Grant to translate Aleksandra Lun's *The Palimpsests*. Other translations from Spanish include Claudia Salazar Jiménez's *Blood of the Dawn*, winner of the 2014 Americas Prize. Her debut novel, *From Here On, Monsters*, is out with Picador.

A NOTE ON THE TYPE

THE TEXT of *The Palimpsests* has been set in a digital revival of American Type Founders' acclaimed Garamond type face. Produced by Mark van Bronkhorst as Garamond ATF Text, the original ATF Garamond was one of the early type revivals of the 20th century by ATF in 1917. Drawn by Morris Fuller Benton with the help of designer and illustrator Thomas Maitland Cleland, ATF Garamond is based on the types cut by Jean Jannon, the *"Caractères de l'Université"* held in Paris at the Imprimerie Nationale. The ATF foundry revival was an extremely popular cut of the face; so much so that their version was licensed by Mergentahler Linotype and issued for hot metal composition as Garamond No. 3 around 1925. This MVB revival seeks to revitalize the more robust appearance of the original metal-era letterpress face which was lost in many of the digital revivals as "fonts" supplanted physical type faces in the 1980s and '90s.

The title, folios, chapter numbers, and opening initials are set in Narziß, designed by Walter Tiemann for the type foundry Gebr. Klingspor of Offenbach, Germany in 1921. Tiemann took his cue from the decorated faces offered by Pierre Simon Fournier in his specimen of types, the *Manuel Typographique* of 1764.

DESIGNED BY MICHAEL BABCOCK

Badenheim 1939 by Aharon Appelfeld
translated by Dalya Bilu
152 PAGES; SC; *391-9; $15.95

The Lonely Years, 1925–1939
by Isaac Babel
translated by A. R. MacAndrew & Max Hayward
432 PAGES; SC; 978-7; $15.95

Tartar Steppe by Dino Buzzati
translated by Stuart C. Hood
212 PAGES; SC; *304-9; $17.95

Sleet by Stig Dagerman
translated by Steven Hartman
240 PAGES; SC; *446-6; $17.95

Wedding Worries by Stig Dagerman
translated by Paul Norlen with Lo Dagerman
256 PAGES; SC; *615-6; $18.95

The Obscene Bird of Night by José Donoso
translated by Hardie St. Martin & Leonard Mades
448 PAGES; SC; *046-8; $19.95

Bloodlines by Marcello Fois
translated by Silvester Mazzarella
288 PAGES; SC; *585-2; $18.95

The Roots of Heaven by Romain Gary
translated by Jonathan Griffin
348 PAGES; SC; *626-2; $18.95

Fortuny by Pere Gimferrer
translated by Adrian West
136 PAGES; SC; *550-0; $17.95

The Parable of the Blind
by Gert Hofmann
translated by Christopher Middleton
152 PAGES; SC; *563-0; $17.95

Desert by J. M. G. Le Clézio
translated by C. Dickson
360 PAGES; SC; *387-2; $18.95

The Prospector by J. M. G. Le Clézio
translated by Carol Marks
352 PAGES; HC; 976-3; $24.95
352 PAGES; SC; *380-3; $16.95

Honeymoon by Patrick Modiano
translated by Barbara Wright
128 PAGES; HC; 947-3; $22.95
128 PAGES; SC; *538-8; $16.95

Missing Person by Patrick Modiano
translated by Daniel Weissbort
192 PAGES; SC; *281-3; $16.95

Five Women by Robert Musil
translated by Eithne Wilkins & Ernst Kaiser
224 PAGES; SC; *401-5; $16.95

I Remember by Georges Perec
translated by Philip Terry
176 PAGES; SC; *517-3; $16.95

Life A User's Manual by Georges Perec
translated by David Bellos
680 PAGES; SC; *373-5; $22.95

Things: A Story of the Sixties & A Man Asleep
by Georges Perec
translated by David Bellos & Andrew Leak
224 PAGES; SC; *157-1; $17.95

Thoughts of Sorts by Georges Perec
translated by David Bellos
160 PAGES; SC; *362-9; $16.95

Three by Georges Perec
translated by Ian Monk
208 PAGES; SC; *254-7; $16.95

A Void by Georges Perec
translated by Gilbert Adair
304 PAGES; SC; *296-7; $17.95

W, or The Memory of Childhood
by Georges Perec, translated by David Bellos
176 PAGES; SC; *158-8; $17.95

Poil de Carrote by Jules Renard
translated by Ralph Manheim
200 PAGES; SC; *523-4; $17.95

The Inner Sky by Rainer Maria Rilke
translated by Damion Searls
192 PAGES; SC; *388-9; $17.95

On Heroes and Tombs by Ernesto Sabato
translated by Helen Lane
480 PAGES; SC; *596-8; $20.95

The Forty Days of Musa Dagh by Franz Werfel
translated by Geoffrey Dunlop
revised by James Reidel
936 PAGES; SC; *407-7; $22.95

The Temple of Iconoclasts
by J. Rodolfo Wilcock
translated by Lawrence Venuti
224 PAGES; SC; *530-2; $17.95

NB: *The* ISBN *prefix for titles with an * is 978-1-56792. The prefix for all others is 978-0-87923.*

If your bookstore does not carry a particular title, you may order it directly from
the publisher by calling 1-800-344-4771, emailing order@godine.com,
or by sending prepayment for the price of the books desired, plus $5 postage & handling, to:
DAVID R. GODINE, PUBLISHER
Post Office Box 450, Jaffrey, New Hampshire 03452 • *www.godine.com*